FOLLOW
the
LEADER

FOLLOW
the
LEADER

LOREE LOUGH

WHITAKER
HOUSE

FOLLOW THE LEADER
(Also included in *Tales of the Heart: 3-in-1 Collection*)

Loree Lough
www.loreelough.com

ISBN: 978-1-60374-630-4
Printed in the United States of America
© 1995, 2010 by Loree Lough

Whitaker House
1030 Hunt Valley Circle
New Kensington, PA 15068
www.whitakerhouse.com

This book has been printed digitally and produced in a standard specification in order to ensure its continuing availability.

Dedication

First, to my faithful readers, whose support and faith keep me writing.

*Second, to Larry, light of my life and stirrer
of my soul, for whom I'm happy to obey
1 Corinthians 7:10: "Let not the wife depart from her husband."*

*Special mention to my wonderful editor,
Courtney, and the ever-capable Lois.*

*Finally, to my once abused, now spoiled dog, who put aside his Frisbee
addiction long enough for me to write these stories!*

Chapter One

September 1868
Freeland, Michigan

H up! Two, three, four. Hup! Two, three, four."

The troops obediently followed their leader, who was walking backward and giving instructions in singsong.

Focusing on something behind the leader, the shortest soldier said, "Uh, Sergeant?"

"No talking in formation," the commander growled playfully.

"But, sir, there's—"

"No 'buts,' recruit. Remain in formation or—"

Thump.

He turned to see what he'd hit—a tick too late to stop what the collision had started.

The shortest soldier plowed into the leader, the two behind him marched into each other, and the young woman, arms moving like windmills, landed on her derriere amid a tangle of skirts as books, slates, and chalk rained down around her.

"Oh, bother!" he said, whipping the cap from his head. "I—I'm sorry, ma'am. Didn't see you standing there. I—we...." He extended a hand to help her up. "Are you all right?"

"Oh, I think I'll live," she said, taking his hand. Brushing dust and grit from her blue velvet skirt, she smiled. "If it'll make you feel better, you and your little army can help me pick up my things."

Had she—had she *winked* at him? No woman, not even Rita, had ever done that before!

He looked at her then. Really looked at her. She had the loveliest smile he'd ever seen. It brightened her big, green eyes, and everything else around her, too. It took a great deal of concentration to look away from the delicate face to fulfill her request, but he found the presence of mind to begin stacking books in his arms. One by one, each item disappeared into her seemingly bottomless canvas bag.

He felt obliged to explain—if not for this adorable young woman, then to encourage good manners in his children, who'd clustered around him, watching closely. Clearing his throat, he ran a hand through his hair and grinned. "We play 'soldier' on family outings," he began. "It helps me keep 'em together. I'm afraid I simply wasn't looking where I was going."

She peered around him at the inquisitive faces of his children. "No harm done," she said.

"C'mere, kids," he instructed them, placing one hand on the blond boy's shoulder. "The little fella here is Timmy." His free hand rested on top of the girl's head. "This pretty brunette is Tricia, and the big guy's name is Tyler."

The woman slung the bag handles over her shoulder. "It's a pleasure to meet all of you," she told the children. "And it was an experience," she added, looking directly into his eyes, "meeting you." She held out one white-gloved hand. "I'm Valerie Carter."

First, she'd winked, and now she was offering her hand? He'd never met a woman quite like her before. Tentatively, he shook it. "Paul Collins," he said, still wondering why her name sounded so familiar.

They stood in silence for a moment, staring into each other's eyes, her hand nearly hidden in his. Timmy coughed. Tricia sighed. Tyler cleared his throat. All three children were grinning when Paul glanced over at them, reminding him to release her hand. "Were you on your way in or out when I—"

"In," she said. "I'm trying to get a head start." Valerie paused, as if wondering whether or not to tell him more. Then, she shrugged and began her explanation. "I'm the new teacher. Monday will be my first day."

His dark eyes widened, and his eyebrows rose. "Well, now, isn't that a coincidence?" he asked his children. "Miss Carter is new here, too." Paul faced her again. "We just came back to town, ourselves. That's why we're here—to enroll the children in school."

She gave the children her friendliest smile, then gathered her skirts and started up the steps of the schoolhouse. "Let's go inside," she suggested, "and get better acquainted." The huge brass doorknob squealed as she turned it, and the heavy oak door creaked as it swung open.

"It's very dark in there," Timmy whispered, staying close to his father's side. "How will I ever learn to read, Pa, if I can't even see the books?"

Valerie's merry laughter brightened the room even before she struck a match to light a lantern. Adjusting the flame, she said, "How's that, Tim?"

The boy grinned shyly and shoved both hands deep in his pockets. "Lots better, ma'am."

"Don't you just hate rainy days?" she asked Tricia. "They're so...." Valerie paused, wrinkling her nose as she searched for the word that best fit the day's mood. "They're so gloomy."

"Yes, ma'am," the girl agreed, focusing on the scuffed toes of her high-buttoned shoes.

Valerie unceremoniously plopped her bag onto the dusty desktop. "This is my first visit to the school, too, you know." Her hands on her hips, she surveyed the one-room space. "Now, where do you suppose the 'brand-new student' forms are?" she asked no one in particular. Rummaging through drawers and shuffling with shelf contents, she frowned. Then, clapping her hands once, she said, "Guess we're just going to have to make one of our own."

She pulled out the battered wooden chair behind her desk and sat down. Taking a sheet of paper and a pencil from her bag, she gestured toward the neat rows of desks. "Please, won't you all sit down?"

Obediently, each Collins did as she'd instructed, including Paul, whose knees nearly touched his earlobes as he tried to balance his considerable frame on the tiny wooden chair.

"What's your full name?" Valerie asked Tyler.

Sitting up straight, the boy said in the deepest voice he could muster, "Tyler Joshua Collins, ma'am."

"What a fine, strong name."

The serious face brightened. "Pa says I'm strong as a horse."

"That's good to know. It'll be good to have a strong young man around to carry in wood when the snow comes. Would you mind being my helper?"

A grin curved his lips upward. "Not at all, ma'am."

"How old are you, Tyler?"

"Be eleven soon, ma'am."

"Let's see," she said, squinting and tapping her chin with the end of her pencil. "That should put you in level five. Maybe even six. Am I right?"

"Yes, ma'am. I finished my fifth year up in York."

"Pennsylvania?"

The boy nodded. "I was born here in Maryland, but we moved to Pennsylvania when I was one."

She smiled. "I guess you don't remember much about it, then, do you?"

Tyler grinned. "Don't remember a thing."

"We have something in common, because I don't know anything about Freeland, either." She met Tricia's eyes next. "If I had to guess, I'd say you're about nine. Am I close?"

Her head bobbed up and down. "I'm eight. Almost." Glancing at her father, she added, "Pa says I'm big for my age. Gonna be tall, like Ma was."

Like Ma *was?* Valerie pretended not to have heard the obvious reference to a deceased mother. Her heart ached for the children. For their father, too. She knew how much it hurt to lose a loved one, but to have lost someone as important as a mother at such a young age…. "You're in your third year, then?"

Tricia nodded. "That's what the teacher back home said."

"This is home now," Timmy pointed out.

Valerie couldn't help but notice the sadness that enveloped the little family at the boy's simple statement. She wondered what event had inspired the move from Pennsylvania to Maryland. "That leaves you, Timmy," she said, her voice deliberately cheery to change the mood. "Have you gone to school before?"

"No, ma'am."

"Level one, then," she said, smiling. Turning her attention to their father, Valerie added, "Mr. Collins, you can be very proud of them. They're fine, mannerly children."

"Thank you for the compliment, ma'am, but Mrs. Collins is responsible for their good behavior." His voice was a near whisper when he said, "She died during the war. I, u…I expect that'll be helpful information if you're to deal with my young'uns on a daily basis."

Suddenly, she felt the need to busy her hands and began rearranging things on her desk. Yes, it was helpful information. These children would most definitely need extra care and compassion. A little more of her time than the children who had two parents.… When she met his eyes again, she said, "I'm sorry to hear of your loss."

Valerie didn't know it was possible to feel so many emotions at once. She experienced confusion, embarrassment, and pity all at the same time.

He grinned sheepishly, twisting his soft, black hat in his hands. "I've had nearly five years to get used to the fact. I suppose I could have put it a bit more gently.…"

"Mr. Collins, there's absolutely no need to apologize. That horrible war.…" Valerie's voice trailed off as she pictured her home, destroyed and smoldering. "The War Between the States cost me everything I held dear. Freeing the slaves was the only good thing to come of it, in my opinion, and if you ask me, the pigheaded menfolk who run this country should have been able to accomplish that without so much bloodshed!"

"Ma was gonna get us a baby," Timmy interjected, "but she had to give it back to God."

Just when you think you're the only one in pain, Valerie said to herself, *someone comes along and shows you things could be worse.*

"God must'a liked Ma a lot," Timmy added, "'cause He kept her and the baby, too."

From the corner of her eye, Valerie saw Paul sit a bit straighter in the tiny chair. Saw him throw back his broad shoulders. That he'd reacted physically to the plain truth five years after his wife's death told Valerie the wound was still quite painful.

She wished for the courage to look him straight in the eye and tell him he'd done a fine job being both father and mother to his children, that the proof glowed in their loving eyes. She wanted to tell him that she'd known men in similar circumstances who had moved heaven and earth to replace their deceased wives as soon as humanly possible.

Valerie glanced at the books on the corner of a desk that desperately needed dusting. At the windows, which probably hadn't been washed in years. At the large, faded blackboard in the corner, which could use a good scrubbing. The floor was gritty with dirt, and the desks and benches…. She had a lot to do, and very little time in which to do it. "Well," she said, standing up, "I have enough information for now. I'll see you all on Monday, bright and early, right?"

"Right," Timmy said, his voice shrill with eagerness.

"Do you have slates?" she asked as she escorted them to the exit.

The children nodded. "Pa made us pack 'em real careful so they wouldn't break during the move," Timmy offered. "Ma bought 'em for us with her egg money before…."

Valerie put her hand on the boy's shoulder, sensing he couldn't complete the awful sentence. "Good! Then I'll see to it that each of you gets a brand-new piece of chalk first thing Monday morning," she said. "We'll consider it my 'welcome back to Freeland' gift to you."

"I think we'd better head on home," Paul told the children, "and let Miss Carter get busy putting her school in order." He opened the door. "Thanks for your help," he said, setting the felt hat atop his head.

She watched them walk down the steps and across the dusty road before they disappeared into the woods just north of town.

The clouds that had darkened the sky earlier were gone now, and the sun shone in the September sky, brightening the day and her spirits alike. Taking a deep breath, Valerie headed back inside to survey what Mr. Collins had called "her school." In two short days, the empty seats would be filled with children.

Valerie's heart beat a bit faster at the prospect of being the person who'd teach them to appreciate all the wonderful things an education could add to their lives. If she could make a positive difference in even one young life, she'd have earned her salary.

She had no way of knowing that she'd already made a difference in three young lives...and one older one....

"She's mighty pretty, Pa. Do you s'pose she's a good teacher?"

Paul thrust his hands deep into his pockets. "She seems real smart to me, Tim." He walked behind his children, picturing their new teacher's happy face. Hearing her light, melodic laughter. Wondering whether her chestnut-colored hair felt as soft as it looked. And pondering what sadness had dimmed the gleam in those big, green eyes. It surprised him to realize he wished he was a boy in school again.

The children ran on ahead, toward their new home. The house hadn't been occupied in years, but Paul and the children had made it livable. Each had worked in a specific room, scrubbing and sweeping until the place sparkled. Still, despite the cleanliness, something was missing....

Paul had wandered the rooms alone each night, listening to the rhythmic sounds of his slumbering children and trying to determine exactly what he'd neglected to do, what he'd forgotten to bring with them from York that would make this house a home, like the one in Pennsylvania had been. They'd been in Freeland for nearly a month, yet he hadn't been able to find that missing piece to the puzzle.

He sat down in front of the hearth with his Bible open on his lap, distracted by the soft, soothing spatter of rain against the windowpanes. Paul leaned back in the creaking rocker and closed his eyes, remembering how, on nights like this, Rita would sit across from him, knitting or darning socks, while he whittled a toy for the children or repaired a harness, both totally content and at peace with their lives. The ache of missing her throbbed harder than ever in this new-yet-old place, and Paul wiped the annoying tear that rolled down his cheek.

He was tired. So very tired. Even his sigh, as silent as the rain-drops that slid down the windowpane, sounded tired.

But he hated the thought of going to bed. Climbing onto the narrow feather mattress alone roused an ache deep inside him that hurt every bit as much as a hammer's blow. He'd lie there, hour after hour, praying that sleep would rescue him from his loneli-ness, from his memories.

But it wouldn't.

And so, Paul had developed a ritual to avoid retiring for the night—one that involved closing windows, locking doors, turn-ing down lanterns, and checking on the children. When the last chin had been tucked in, though, he'd have to admit that with the sunrise would come the promise of a long day's work. He needed his sleep, he knew, and so, reluctantly, he'd slip between the crisp, white sheets that Rita had embroidered with bright blue flowers, remembering that she was gone forever.

Now, Paul glanced around the room that he'd shared with her during those first happy months of their ten-year marriage. They'd lived on the old Collins farm barely two years when Rita's father had suffered a heart attack. If she and Paul hadn't returned to Pennsylvania to help out, the old man would surely have lost his farm and also his life. Paul had rented the Collins property to a friend, who was to see that things were cared for until he and Rita could return. How could he have known that the return to Maryland would never happen in her lifetime?

Their years in Pennsylvania had been happy ones, thanks especially to Rita. Knowing how her husband missed his family, and how it must have hurt him to have left the farm behind, she'd worked diligently to make the dark, drafty house beside her father's a warm, bright place. With Rita beside him, Paul had barely noticed the faded wallpaper or the imperfections in the windowpanes that distorted their view of the fields beyond.

But after that soldier's bullet had ended her life, the house had seemed to shriek with flaws and failings. Rooms that had felt light and airy thanks to Rita's ruffles and embroidery turned instantly gloomy. In place of her sweet greeting at the end of a long, hard day, Paul heard groaning floorboards and squealing hinges. Instead of the aromas of sweetbreads and hearty soups, the musty smell of grit met him at the door. He couldn't bear life in Pennsylvania without her.

He prayed that in Freeland, where their love had begun, he could come to terms with a widower's lifestyle.

He quickly discovered that the little house hadn't changed in the ten years they'd lived up north. It was still sturdy and strong, and he'd tried to arrange the furniture inside it as Rita might have, hoping it would bring him peace and contentment in those solitary hours after the children were asleep.

But nothing he did eased the ache or made him miss her less. Except for the warmth of his children's love, his world was mostly cold now.

And Paul doubted that anything would ever truly warm him again.

The sun had just peeked over the hilltop when he heard their voices. Having been up for hours, he had already milked all three cows, gathered a dozen eggs, and fed the two horses. It was time to replace that slat in the barnyard fence; he'd work until the children called to him.

They'd no doubt found the pan of biscuits warming on the stovetop and the pot of oatmeal beside it. They'd eaten and dressed, performed their indoor chores, and then come running, as Rita had taught them to do every morning, pretending they had no idea where he might be. *Praise the Lord*, he thought, *that some things, at least, never change.*

From where he stood, high atop a grassy knoll overlooking Freeland's town square, Paul could see the white church steeple gleaming in the morning sunlight. He remembered helping his father hang the old bronze bell; remembered, too, helping replace the greased paper in the arched windows with colorful panes of beveled glass.

Paul shook his head sadly. The memory of it ached, even after so many years had passed. He sent a prayer heavenward, thanking God that his father hadn't lived to face the fact that his only son didn't want to walk in his footsteps. If only Paul could have spared his mother the same pain.

"Fine! Hire a new pastor if you like," she'd cried, weeks after his father's funeral. "I can't bear to stay if you won't be in charge." And with that, she'd made arrangements to return to Chicago, where she'd been living with her sister ever since.

He'd never explained his reluctance to stand behind the pulpit to his mother—or anyone else, for that matter—partly because she hadn't asked, and partly because he didn't completely understand it himself. Paul didn't know what God had planned for his life, but he did know what God *didn't* intend for him to do....

The day before their wedding, Rita had tearfully confessed, "I'm not good enough to be a pastor's wife. Planning luncheons and church socials, counseling and helping, nursing and teaching...." Giggling past her tears, she'd blushed and hugged him. "I'm too selfish to share you!"

"Our love isn't selfish," he'd assured her. And nearly every day of their marriage, they'd comment on how much they cherished their time alone as the playful debate seesawed: Did she love her role as wife and mother more than he loved his position as husband and father?

A clap of thunder slapped him rudely back to the present. He'd been letting his mind wander again—something he'd been doing a lot of since Rita's death. But it was no wonder, when everything, it seemed, reminded him of her. He went back to working on the fence.

"Pa!" Timmy called. "Where are you?"

He leaned on the shovel and rubbed his stubbled chin, glad to have his mind solidly back in the present and far from the haunting, hurtful memories of Rita. "Over here, son."

The boy ran up and threw his arms around Paul's waist. "Breakfast was delicious, Pa. Every time I eat one of your biscuits, I wonder how you learned to cook so good."

Paul let the grammar error slide. "It's your ma's recipe." Even that reminded him of how much he missed her, for she'd insisted he learn the basics of cooking and cleaning and shopping. "You must always be prepared," she'd said, "for what lies ahead." It was as though she'd known, somehow, that he'd need those skills someday. Silently, he thanked her, then wished her from his mind. He waited for the pain to subside, though he didn't really expect it to. Five years of experience had taught him that no amount of wishing or hoping or praying could blot her from his memory.

The children came home from school chattering and giggling, sounding happier than they had in a very long time. During supper, all they could talk about was school. And Miss Carter.

"She has green eyes, Pa," Timmy said. "I never saw eyes that color before."

Paul nodded, remembering that he'd had a similar thought in front of the schoolhouse after knocking her down. Eyes as green and bright and shimmering as emeralds....

"And when the sun shines on her hair, it looks like a copper kettle, but in the schoolhouse, it's brown." Timmy pursed his lips, trying to find a color that would explain his teacher's hair. "It reminds me of—"

"Chestnuts," Paul said, absently stirring a spoonful of sugar into his coffee.

Timmy nodded, then propped his elbow on the table, resting his chin on a chubby fist. "I wish I was old like you, Pa."

Paul met his youngest son's eyes and laughed. "And why is that, Tim?"

"'Cause then I could ask her to marry me." The boy sighed. "She's the most beautiful lady I've ever seen."

Up to that point, Tyler hadn't said a word about Miss Carter. "Ma was prettier," he said now. "Her hair was the color of wheat fields, and her eyes were bluer than the sky."

Paul's heart pounded as he thought, *And her smile as sweet as the angels' in heaven....*

Suddenly, Timmy's eyes filled with tears. "Why can't I remember Ma?"

Paul placed his hand over the boy's. "You're trying too hard, Tim." He looked to heaven for the strength to say what his son needed to hear. Pressing his big hand over the boy's heart, he said, "Your ma is there, deep inside you."

"But shouldn't I be able to remember her all the time?"

At that moment, Paul envied his son a little bit, for he'd have given the best tooth in his head to get through just one day without memories of Rita assaulting his mind. "Now, what's this?" Paul asked, wiping a tear from the child's cheek. "My big boy, crying?"

"I'm not a big boy!" Timmy shouted, burying his face in the crook of his arm. "I'm only six, and I want my ma!"

Paul stood up and lifted Timmy's chin, then squatted beside the table to make himself child-sized. "Tim," he said in a soothing voice, "your ma is happy with God in heaven, and she wants us to be happy, too, right here, together."

The boy leaned against his father's massive chest. "What's God want our ma for, anyway?" he demanded. "He's got all those angels to keep Him company. He doesn't need her, but we do!"

Tyler put his arm around his brother's shoulders. "We all miss her," he said, sounding much older than his years, "but it's like Pa said: she's happy in heaven. She doesn't want to come back, so we have to learn to live without her."

Paul met his oldest son's gaze, then looked at Tricia's sad face. Clearly, she agreed with her older brother.

"Is that what you've thought all this time?" he asked them. "You've thought your ma *wanted* to leave us?"

The children said nothing but stared blankly at their half-emptied plates.

Paul stood up again and walked to the fireplace. *Lord,* he prayed silently, *help me comfort them*…. When he faced them again, he spoke softly: "Your ma never would have left you by choice. She loved the three of you more than life itself." *Right up until that soldier's bullet ripped through her,* he ranted mentally.

"You told her to stay inside, where it was safe. If she hadn't gone out there to get the quilt from the clothesline…." His daughter stamped one foot. "She should have loved us *more* than that dumb old thing, even if her mother *did* make it."

Tricia was right, and he'd had the same thought a thousand times since that awful day. It was good, he realized, that the children's true feelings were finally coming out. He held out his arms, and they filled them. Blinking back hot tears, he whispered hoarsely, "I'm sure if she'd known what was out there, she wouldn't have gone outside," he said. "She never would have willingly left you, especially not for a dumb old quilt."

He kissed Tricia's cheek, then said, "Tyler's right. We all miss her." Clearing his throat, he closed his eyes and prayed for the strength to say what had to be said, once and for all: "It's time to get on with our lives. She would have wanted it that way." He paused, hugged the three of them tightly, and added, "Why don't we start by getting these dishes cleaned up?"

Tricia moved first, followed by Tyler, and, finally, Timmy.

Paul slumped into the rocker and picked up his Bible. "You shouldn't have talked about Ma," he heard Tricia whisper to her brothers. "It makes Pa sad. Every time one of you brings up her name, he looks like he's going to cry." She concluded by saying, "We all miss her, but he misses her even more."

It seemed all he did lately was pretend. He pretended to be strong for the children. Pretended he didn't miss Rita so much that it ached. Now, he pretended he hadn't heard Tricia's remarks.

Her words, like a cold slap in the face, made him face the hard truth. He didn't want to believe he'd been so lost in his own misery and grief that he hadn't seen how deeply Rita's death had affected the children. But Tricia's words were proof that he'd been wallowing so long in a deep sea of self-pity that he'd seen only his own pain.

Rita had told him once that he could do anything he set his mind to, and with her encouragement and love, he'd believed it. Without her, however, he was unsure, afraid of the future. So, he'd returned to Freeland, where they'd started their happy life together, hoping to reclaim some of that certainty and joy. What he hadn't realized until Tricia's little speech was that he'd been looking straight at happiness all along—in the loving eyes of his children.

Trust the Lord, he told himself, *and He'll pull you through, just as He's done since you were a boy.* He turned to 1 Corinthians 10:13 and silently read, *"God is faithful, who will not suffer you to be tempted above that ye are able; but will with the temptation also make a way to escape, that ye may be able to bear it."*

Leaning back in the rocking chair, Paul smiled. And for perhaps the first time since Rita's death, he wasn't the least bit tempted to feel sorry for himself.

Chapter Two

S he hadn't expected to like Freeland.

Richmond was home. Had always been home, even after she'd buried her family, even after she'd walked away from the smoldering remains of what had been Carter Hall.

The very idea of leaving Virginia had terrified her, but Valerie had grown weary of struggling to survive on meager wages, having been born into luxury and having lived most of her life surrounded by elegance. Teaching in Freeland's one-room schoolhouse would certainly prove an easier life than waiting tables in the swank Southern Belle Hotel, so, at her cousin Sally's advice and insistence, she'd headed north to Maryland.

Freeland was the town that, decades ago, had become home to Valerie's favorite uncle. He'd spent most of his life traveling throughout the eastern countryside, peddling his adaptation of the grist mill. He had been on his way home from demonstrating the handy contraption at a county fair when his carriage had overturned, pinning him underneath.

Valerie's Aunt Betsy had become a rich widow on that terrible, stormy night. Alone and afraid, she'd returned to Richmond. Just as Richmond was the place of Betsy's roots, Freeland was the only home Sally had ever known. Just weeks before her father's tragic death, Sally had taken a husband and set up house on the outskirts of town.

It was from Valerie's home in Virginia that Aunt Betsy had written to inform Aunt Sally of the many tragedies that had befallen the Carter family: the deaths of Valerie's father, brothers, and mother; the destruction of their import-export business; the demise of the grand old plantation. Sally must have gotten busy the moment she'd torn open that letter, because before Valerie had received the official invitation to come and teach in Freeland's little school, Sally had already arranged lodging, welcome-to-town visits from neighbors and fellow church members, and a one-way ticket on the Baltimore and Ohio Railroad.

That letter had changed Valerie's entire life, and now she gently tucked it back into her bureau drawer, giggling to herself as she thought of how all of Sally's work would have been for naught if she'd refused to move to Freeland.

Valerie had been born and raised in her father's mansion. The modest cottage, situated just behind the schoolhouse in the center of town, had no pantry, no summer kitchen, no keeping room, no majestic staircase. But Valerie loved it just the same because it was *hers*. She especially loved the wide, covered porch that ran the width of the tiny house, and the first thing she'd done after unpacking her bags that late-August day was to move the comfortable bentwood rockers flanking the flagstone fireplace onto the porch. In Richmond, it had been a Carter family tradition to sit on the veranda after dinner, sipping mint tea as each family member shared in turn the events of his or her day.

And Valerie was continuing the ritual. Each night, after a light supper, she tidied her small kitchen before relaxing beneath the slatted, white-enameled ceiling and listening to the soft sounds of twilight.

Nearly a month had passed since her arrival. She missed Richmond. She missed family gatherings after church on Sundays. She missed Mama and Papa and her brothers, Lee Junior and

Delbert. She missed standing on the docks and inspecting huge crates that bore treasures from the Orient and Africa and Europe. She missed old Garth, whose stories had entertained her from the cradle, and Delilah, who'd been her cook, maid, and dearest friend for as long as she could remember. The old Negro couple had taught Valerie practical things—how to tie a slipknot, how to bake bread—and spiritual things, too—how to say the Lord's Prayer, how to forgive a transgressor.

Her father had owned several thousand acres of land, known throughout the South as Carter's Hall Tobacco Plantation, and it was from his oak-paneled study that he'd run his import-export business. Contrary to Southern tradition, her father had stout-heartedly refused to own slaves. The blacks who'd worked for him had been hired hands, with the same rights and privileges as the whites who'd worked alongside them. They'd been paid fair wages and given clean little homes in which to live, as well as a few acres of good, productive land where they'd raised laying hens, milk cows, and vegetables.

When the War Between the States had broken out, her father had refused to wear a uniform of either color, saying that since the good Lord had seen fit to free him from the bonds of sin, he'd not enslave man, woman, or child of any skin color. The philosophy might have been tolerated up North, but in Richmond, the new Confederate capital, his words were blasphemy.

Her brothers had fought for the South, much to her father's dismay. The only positive thing to come from the day he was shot was her knowledge that he'd never learn they'd both died defending slavery.

On many occasions, Valerie's mother had told her that she'd inherited her father's inner strength—although Valerie had the impression that her mother hadn't intended it as a compliment. That strength had come in handy when she'd packed her few remaining possessions and boarded the Baltimore-bound train. Riding in the jolting, rattling passenger car, she'd silently thanked her father for having instilled in her the ability to accept life—and everything in it—at face value. "Keeps you from going off the deep end, wishing for things that can never be," he'd advised her.

Valerie realized that from the moment she'd stepped off the train, Freeland had lived up to its name; Negro and white, and Spanish and Oriental, lived, worshipped, shopped, and went to school side by side, in peace and harmony. Her father would have loved it here.

Since she would be teaching the children, she'd already met nearly everyone in town; it had taken very little time to feel welcome. In a matter of days, she'd come to view her students like she would her own children. She saw to it that each of them ate a healthy lunch, made sure they were all properly dressed for the weather, and supplied them with slates, chalk, and books. If their parents couldn't afford the tools, Valerie paid for them herself.

In particular, though, Valerie had developed a special fondness for the Collins children. They were intelligent, open-minded youngsters, ready to learn and eager to please. It had become a real struggle not to show favoritism to the three motherless children.

She'd seen their father on only one occasion since the day she'd enrolled his children. He'd come to town one afternoon for supplies and had stopped at the schoolhouse on his way home to have lunch with his children. She remembered the way their faces had lit up at the sight of his large, muscular body filling the doorway. Just as memorable was the adoring expression in his eyes as he'd looked at each one of them.

This was a special man, and Valerie knew it. He worked hard and long in his fields every day, as evidenced by his sun-kissed face and calloused hands. Yet he obviously made time for his children, for Timmy, Tricia, and Tyler seemed to be the happiest, best-behaved, best-adjusted children in the school, despite their tragic loss.

She couldn't deny that Paul was a handsome man, with his huge, soulful, brown eyes and the wild mass of dark curls on his head. If she could change anything about him, Valerie would see to it that he smiled more often, for he was especially good-looking when he did. Perhaps, when she got to know him better, she could find a pleasant, noncommittal kind of way to tell him how his smile affected those around him…but only to encourage him to smile more often, of course.

Enough daydreaming! she scolded herself. *The man has neither the time nor the inclination to notice you, Valerie Ann Carter. With that big farm to run and three kids to raise, it's a wonder he has time left over to breathe!*

The admission didn't stop her from daydreaming, however, and as she listened to the katydids' song and the locusts' twang, she rocked in quiet comfort. Freeland wasn't Virginia or Richmond or even Carter Hall, but it surely had started to feel like *home.*

Rev. Gemmill prayed fervently for the good weather to hold until the annual picnic at St. John's the following Sunday had ended. Early in the week, Valerie spoke to Mrs. Gemmill and asked what she could do to help out.

"Can you cook?" the pastor's wife asked.

"Why, yes. I can."

"Good! We need pies. Lots of 'em. Bake as many as you have time and fixings for. And since you're unmarried, make a box lunch, too. We auction them off, you know, and this year, the money raised will go toward a new organ for the church," Mrs. Gemmill said.

On Monday night, Valerie baked four pies, and on Tuesday, four more. By Friday, fourteen pies lined her table, buffet, and serving cart. Bright and early on Saturday, she fried up an entire chicken, baked fluffy biscuits and a chocolate cake, and whipped up a batch of cider for the boxed lunch. The only container large enough to hold it all was her sewing basket, and she carefully tucked the food items onto the nest she'd made from a red gingham tablecloth. Then, as an afterthought, she tied the whole thing up with a wide, pink satin ribbon.

Now...what to wear to the picnic on Sunday?

Valerie had salvaged only four dresses from the terrible fire that had destroyed Carter Hall. She'd worn the blue one with the white piping along its hem and sleeves nearly every day since school had started. Certainly, the children were as bored looking at it as she was with wearing it....

On the morning of the picnic, she smoothed her pink skirt, adjusted the bow of the matching bonnet, and pretended to listen to Rev. Gemmill's sermon. As the town's schoolmarm, she was more or less expected to be present at Sunday services, so, of course, she'd go through the motions.

Her body would, that is—but her mind and soul would not. If she hadn't been good enough to secure God's ear as she'd begged Him to spare her father's life, to save his business; if she hadn't been good enough to deserve an answer to her pleas for Him to save her mother and her brothers, she certainly wasn't good enough now. So, if a word or a phrase from Scripture managed to weaken her decision not to listen to Him, Valerie focused on other things, like planning a lesson for her students or redesigning a dress. Today, she mentally rearranged the ruffles on her skirt into a bustle in the back....

Valerie's favorite dress was an emerald gown of cotton twill. It had a six-inch flounce at its hem and black velvet swirls on the lapels of the short, matching jacket. The white bodice boasted twin ruffles, as did the long, cuffed sleeves. Tiny pearl buttons formed a delicate flower on the high collar, and a wide, black satin belt, tied in a big bow in the back, draped down the skirt and nearly reached the hem. But it was far too heavy for a picnic.

After church, she'd change into the white eyelet. Simple in material and design, it could be embellished with a colorful apron without looking gaudy. And if she wore it with her navy pinafore, she could carry her threadbare blue purse without looking like a ragamuffin.

It wasn't like Valerie to spend a lot of time in front of the mirror, but she did so this afternoon. This would be her first appearance at an official Freeland event, and she wanted to make a good impression so that Sally and her husband wouldn't be embarrassed for having recommended her for the job as the town's teacher.

Ordinarily, Valerie tucked her long hair into a twist at the nape of her neck. Today, however, she let it fall softly over her shoulders, held back above each ear by her mother's ebony combs. She didn't like to think of herself as a vain woman, but she had a reputation to uphold as the teacher of the community children, so the dab of rose cologne she dotted on her wrists had nothing whatever to do with the possibility that she might have a chance to visit with Paul Collins.

She draped the fraying velvet straps of the drawstring purse over her arm and headed for the kitchen to grab her pies and walk over to the churchyard. At the door, Valerie stopped dead in her tracks. "How ever will you get all these pies to the church?" she wondered aloud.

"It'd be my pleasure to help you," said a deep, resonant voice.

"Mr. Collins!" she said, a trembling hand at her throat.

"Sorry if I startled you." Removing his black cap, he added, "You look mighty pretty today, Miss Carter."

She felt herself blush at his compliment. "I—I was just trying to figure out how I'd get all these pies over to the—"

"So I heard," he interrupted, grinning. "The young'uns suggested we stop by and see if you needed a hand." With a jerk of his thumb, he indicated the wagon behind him, where his children were giggling and wriggling with anticipation of the day ahead.

The schoolhouse was situated down the street from the center of Freeland, where the church, post office, and train station sat on one side of the railroad tracks, the livery stable, feed store, and hotel on the other. It would have been a lovely, quick walk, carrying a pie in each hand. But fourteen pies would require at least seven trips! "I'm much obliged," she said.

Paul opened the creaking screen door and stepped into the clean, sparsely furnished room. "Tyler," he called, "you and Tricia come on in here and help us load these goodies onto the wagon."

The children were beside him in a whipstitch, and Valerie handed them each a gingham cloth-covered pie. "I'm so glad you were thinking of me this morning. I don't know what I'd have done without you!"

Tyler and Tricia exchanged a puzzled glance, then looked at their father, whose flushed cheeks and downcast eyes told Valerie it had been his idea, not the children's, to see if she needed help getting to town. Her heart fluttered in response.

Paul cleared his throat and, balancing a pie on each big hand, held the door open with his elbow. "After you," he said, smiling at her.

Even with three of them, it took two trips to move the desserts from her kitchen to his wagon. "Sakes alive," Timmy said as Paul climbed into the front seat, "how many pies did you bake, Miss Carter?"

Laughing, she said, "Too many!"

"No such thing as too many pies," Paul corrected her, extending a hand to help her up.

She took his hand and, as on the day they'd met, noticed its gentle strength. She took her place beside him, tightly gripping the handles of the basket that held the boxed lunch. A small hope thrummed inside her. *If I were still a praying woman*, she thought, *I'd pray Paul would bid highest on my lunch.* Because, as everybody knew, the lady who had prepared the lunch was obliged to share it with the gentleman who bought it....

Heads turned and whispers floated as they rode into town. "Seems we've set tongues to wagging," Paul observed, a wry grin lifting one corner of his mouth.

It was Valerie's turn to blush. She gripped the basket handles tighter and lifted her chin. "Well! If they've nothing better to discuss than with whom I hitch a ride into town, maybe the reverend can find some chore to occupy their time!"

Valerie thoroughly enjoyed the sound of Paul's laughter, and she decided, right then and there, to make it happen again...and again...by day's end.

Paul parked between two other wagons beside the church, jumped down, and tied his horse to the hitching post. Then, walking around to Valerie's side of the wagon, he reached up, wrapped his big hands around her waist, and put her gently onto the ground. "Now then," he said, "let's see about putting those pies someplace where *we'll* be sure to find them."

Paul, Valerie, and the children headed for the rows of makeshift tables in the churchyard, which the ladies of the parish had covered with tablecloths of every color and pattern. Just beyond stood the food tent, and the foursome deposited Valerie's pies inside. It was during their final trip to the wagon that Paul stopped beside a table that had been set up beneath a large oak. "Is this one to your liking?" he asked Valerie.

When she'd spotted it on their first pass, Valerie had thought it would make for the perfect place to enjoy the meal, and she might have suggested it to him…if it wouldn't have seemed terribly forward and presumptuous. For all she knew, he'd already planned to share the day with someone, but knowing *she* was that someone made her heart beat doubly fast. "This is just fine," she said. "There's a lovely breeze, and plenty of shade," she rambled, "and we're just near enough to the food and the band."

The musicians were adjusting their fiddle strings and tuning their guitars just beyond the clearing. Paul glanced in their direction and grinned. "So we are," he said. "So we are."

All morning, as she visited with her students and their families, Valerie found herself looking for Paul. It never took more than a few moments to spot him, for he stood head and shoulders above the rest of the crowd. Once, as she was scanning the faces in search of his, she caught him staring at her, and she had to remind herself what she'd read about deep breathing being the latest cure for shortness of breath. Valerie inhaled a huge gulp of air, held her breath, then exhaled slowly. Yes, her heart had indeed ceased its nonsensical fluttering, but whether it was because she'd practiced the latest in medical advice or because Paul had focused his attention elsewhere, Valerie didn't know.

Rev. Gemmill put an end to her wondering when he began marching through the crowd, banging a soup ladle on the bottom of a pot. "Attention, everyone! May I have your attention, please?" The round-faced preacher hopped onto the platform at the front of the food tent and waved his arms high in the air. "It's time for the most highly anticipated event at our annual picnics," he announced, a big grin on his pink-cheeked face. "The boxed lunch auction!"

Whistles, applause, and hoots of pleasure resounded through the churchyard.

"Now, now," he said good-naturedly, "let's keep it down, or we'll never get this over with. Mrs. Gemmill," he said, gesturing for his wife to join him, "won't you hand me the first lunch?"

The stout little woman marched up the steps, stood beside her husband, and lifted the first lunch from the table beside her: a tidy white container tied up with a big red bow. "Lucy Johnson made this one," she said, holding it up for the crowd's inspection.

"Now, let's not forget that the bidding is open to unmarried gentlemen only," the pastor chided, a teasing glint in his eye. "I'll open the bidding at five cents."

"Ten cents," called Charlie Smith, his forefinger in the air.

"Fifteen!" countered Bill Brown, waving his straw hat.

The lunch sold for fifty cents, and a blushing Lucy Johnson left the tent on the arm of a strutting Seth Powell.

When eight lunches had been sold, Valerie realized that she didn't know how many unmarried folks lived in Freeland. Suddenly, she wished she'd paid more attention to Paul and less to the activities, for she had no idea how many boxes he'd bid on.

Suddenly, Valerie saw her own basket lifted up by Mrs. Gemmill. "Goodness, this thing weighs a ton!" she said, laughing. "What's in here, girl, salted rocks?" When the laughter died down, she added, "This lunch was prepared by our very own lovely schoolteacher, Miss Valerie Carter."

"Well," the pastor said, "since it outweighs all the others by half, I'll start the bidding at ten cents."

"Thirty!" hollered Bertram Johansen.

Tom Lowe shouted, "Thirty-five!"

"Three dollars," said a deep voice from the back of the crowd.

Muffled whispers and gasps floated forward as the shock of the high bid sank in.

"Did I hear *three dollars?*" the reverend asked.

Heads turned as the parishioners searched for the man who'd offered to pay such a steep price for a simple boxed lunch.

"You heard right," said the voice.

"Why, Paul Collins," said Mrs. Gemmill, "I was wondering why you hadn't bid on any of the others. Have a hankerin' for salted rocks, do you?"

Laughing heartily, Rev. Gemmill held the basket high. "Sold," he said, "to the man with the big, fat wallet!"

When Paul met her gaze, Valerie knew in an instant that while she'd been watching the auction, he'd been watching *her.* She smiled and willed her heart to stop racing as he made his way through the crowd.

"Guess they'll want us up there," he said, his voice so quiet and shy it reminded her of Tyler's. Without warning, he grabbed her hand and led her to the platform. Just before they reached it, he leaned close to her ear and whispered, "Fried chicken is my all-time favorite."

She read the teasing glint in his dark eyes and smiled. "How'd you know what was in my basket?"

"I can smell my favorite meal a mile off." Then, he got into the short line of fellows who'd bought lunches, grinning at the good-natured taunts of his fellow Freelanders.

"You're mighty generous," Valerie said when at last they sat down at their table. "Why, I'll be the talk of the town since my lunch went for more than twice what any of the others—"

"Let's just hope it tastes as good as it smells," Paul said in a teasing glint in his eyes.

Unable to continue looking into those big, brown eyes, Valerie glanced around. "Where do you suppose the children are?" she asked, spreading a fuzzy blanket of red plaid on the ground.

Paul nodded toward the trees. "Over there, eating pie."

Smiling, she knelt beside him and began taking things from the basket: chicken, buttered biscuits, sweet pickles, chocolate cake. "I hope you like the cider," she said, sitting back on her heels. "It's my mother's recipe, and she didn't use much sugar. It may seem a bit tart if you're used to—"

"If it isn't sweet enough," he said, "all I'll need to do is look at you."

She'd just placed a red-and-white checkered napkin across her lap, and in response to his unexpected compliment, her hands froze in the middle of smoothing it. "So tell me, Mr. Collins, how you ended up in York, Pennsylvania."

"Went up there ten years ago," he said, biting into a drumstick, "when my wife's father needed help running his farm. It was supposed to be a temporary move, but he never really recovered." He tore off a piece of a biscuit and popped it into his mouth. "I hear you're from Richmond?"

She nodded. "My great-uncle helped found Freeland."

"Is that so?" Paul studied her face for a moment. "My mother was born here."

"He talked about Freeland every time he visited. Perhaps I'll recognize her name...."

"Leila," he said, almost reverently. "Leila Morris."

"Was she any relation to Isaac Morris?"

He grinned at her excitement. "He was her great-grandfather. Why?"

"Isaac Morris once owned all this land." Her hand waved across the lawn. "Everything that's now Freeland, and everything that surrounds it. He sold it to John Freeland in 1790. Mr. Freeland opened the first general store. The first post office...."

Valerie continued, thrilled to have someone to share her love of history with, to know someone who seemed as interested in it as she. "Mr. Hoffman at the general store told me that his family owned the first paper mill here. Did you know the Hoffman Mill sold the government the paper on which our first currency was printed?"

"Well, I'll be." Paul continued to study her flashing, intelligent eyes; her lilting, cheery voice; the feminine way she sat there, her legs tucked beneath her on the blanket; the delicate way she nibbled at her chicken and sipped her cider. After a moment, Paul blinked, realizing he'd been staring.

"I'm sorry. I'm boring you," she laughed.

"I'm not the least bit bored," he admitted easily, helping himself to a chicken thigh from the basket. "Seems to me you're just the type to be teaching our children."

She met his eyes. "Why, thank you, Mr. Collins."

He wanted to tell her to call him Paul. Paul *darling*. Grinning, he said, "I was just stating a fact. And please, call me Paul."

It wasn't until the pastor announced the last square dance that Paul and Valerie realized their lunch had lasted two hours. Quickly, they shoved the remaining food and utensils back into the basket and folded the blanket. "Do you like hoedowns, Mr. Collins? I mean—Paul?"

The mischievous glint in her eyes made him grin. "I don't mind 'em, I suppose, but I'm afraid I'm not very good at dancin'."

She rested the basket against the trunk of the tree they u been sitting under and held out her hand. "Well, why not let me be the judge of that?"

He'd never met a woman like her. If there was a thought in her head, it popped right out of her mouth. She had a mind of her own, that was for certain! Paul put his hand in hers and let her lead him to the dance floor. He felt like a giant beside this petite woman.

As she half ran ahead of him, he watched her purposeful yet feminine stride. Though small-boned and trim-waisted, she was far from delicate. That much was evident in the power of her grip. She moved like a deer, each tiny foot landing precisely where she wanted it to. He paid particular attention to her dainty, white-slippered feet. *Lord,* he prayed, *don't let me step on those tiny toes; I'm liable to mash 'em flat.*

He wondered exactly how old Miss Valerie Carter was. Eighteen? Twenty, perhaps? And then he wondered what a lovely young thing like her saw in a tired old man like him—a thirty-five-year-old widower with more responsibilities on his shoulders than hairs on his head. But before he could formulate an answer, folks had lined up on the planks of the makeshift dance floor. When fiddle, banjo, guitar, and jug played the opening notes to "Old Joe Clark," toes started tapping.

Valerie felt wonderful in his arms. She looked wonderful, too, in her pretty white dress, its full skirt swinging around her slender ankles as she kicked across the floor away from him, then back to him again. He took the other ladies in his arms when the caller said he should, but he paid them no mind. He could think only of when it would be Valerie's turn to dance with him again.

"Swing your partners," the caller sang, "do-si-do."

And they swung and do-si-doed until the music stopped.

"You said you weren't very good," she said, fanning her face with one hand, "but you're a marvelous dancer." She stuck out her foot. "Not one scuff!"

He was laughing. *Laughing*, of all things! That was something he hadn't done since he didn't know when. Paul bowed low. "Thank you, m'lady."

Then, like Cinderella's ball, it was over. Darkness had begun to fall, and with it, the picnic noised quieted. Good-byes and See-you-laters filtered across the church lawn as the parishioners hopped into their wagons and onto their horses and headed home.

"Can we give you a lift?" Paul asked Valerie.

"It's just a short way...."

"But we're going right past your house." He wanted them to spend a few more minutes together, and, judging by the expectant look on her face, so did she.

"Well, I suppose these aren't the most sensible walking shoes."

Relief surged through him as he helped her onto the wagon seat.

"Nice day, wasn't it?" Tyler asked as they rolled slowly up the road.

Paul looked at Valerie and smiled. "Very nice day, son. *Very* nice."

Chapter Three

It was obvious that Paul had no intention of hurrying to Valerie's place. The children, who'd been babbling excitedly when they'd boarded the wagon, now leaned quietly against the rough-hewn sideboards. "All that fun and excitement seems to have tuckered them out," Valerie said, peeking over her shoulder. "Timmy will probably be asleep before you get him into—"

"I hate to see the day end," Paul interrupted her.

She glanced at his profile, silhouetted by the setting September sun. It was a face of angles and planes that served to accent his strength of character. The steady *clip-clop* of the horse's hooves kept time with the crickets' chirps in the field alongside the dusty road, lulling her into a calm, happy mood.

Then his dark eyes met hers. "I can't remember when I've enjoyed a lady's company more."

She held his gaze for a moment, then stared at the now-empty basket on her lap. She wanted to say, "I've *never* enjoyed a man's company more." Instead, she said, "I enjoyed the picnic, too."

His soft chuckle blended with the hoofbeats and insect sounds and owl hoots, reminding her how often he'd laughed as they'd shared her boxed lunch. He'd never met a woman who could mimic cows and birds...and even Rev. Gemmill, and he'd told her so as they were eating. He'd never met one who deliberately made silly faces, either. "All the women I've known," he'd said, "are far too busy trying to impress folks with their proper manners to show the world who they really are. It's as though they don't realize the true definition of etiquette is never making another human being feel uncomfortable." He'd smiled. "I can't count how many times today I saw or heard you put folks at ease." Remembering his words, Valerie was glad for the semidarkness that hid her blush.

She was glad, too, for the comfortable conversation they shared. When he told her how his young wife had been killed, it took every ounce of self-control to keep from giving his hand a sympathetic squeeze. In fact, Valerie came so close to resting her fingertips on his forearm that she could feel the heat of his tanned skin against her palm. But on the chance that he might read the gesture as a show of pity, she held more tightly to the basket handles instead.

Paul, on the other hand, didn't hesitate to grab her hand when she told him that the war had taken her loved ones, the family business, and Carter Hall. "The Lord has surely blessed you with a sturdy constitution," he said, smiling compassionately, "for you've weathered life's storms well."

She wanted to snatch back her hand and say that the Lord had had nothing to do with the person she'd become. Her strength— if, indeed, she possessed any—had been inherited from her father, not granted by God! She'd give Him credit for one thing, and one thing only: allowing everything of value to be stolen from her.

But she didn't snap at Paul, and she didn't take back her hand. The poetry of his words and the warm light from his eyes touched her like few things had before. If she were still a believer, Valerie might have prayed right then and there that God would open this man's heart to her, for she sensed that he had much in common with her father. But thanks to all the death and destruction she'd witnessed, she didn't pray—*wouldn't* pray—because life had taught her the pain that resulted from believing in childish, blind-follower fairy tales.

Logic and reason were what she believed in now. "It is what it is," her father had loved to say, and common sense told her that Paul Collins was kind and compassionate, a loving father, a gentleman. Hard work, drive, and determination were responsible for the man he'd become, not *God*.

She heard him *tsk-tsk* to stop the horse before parking the wagon alongside the white picket gate that opened to her front walk.

"Well, Miss Carter, you're home, I'm sad to say."

Thankfully, night was closing in, for it hid yet another blush. "Thank you so much for the ride. For the lovely time today."

He looked over his shoulder. "You were right," he said, the nod of his head inviting her to peek into the wagon bed. "They're plumb tuckered out."

Valerie smiled at the angelic faces of his sleeping children.

Paul leaned closer and sniffed the air. "Roses?"

Just as he inhaled her sweet scent now, Valerie had inhaled his scents of fresh hay and bath soap all day long. She wanted to close her eyes and take a last long drink of them so that later, when she was alone, she could exhale slowly and remember his crisp, manly musk. Faint shards of moonlight slanted across his chiseled features. She'd never seen longer, thicker eyelashes in her life. And the brown curls that poked out from beneath his cap glimmered with silvery highlights. Valerie warned herself to tread carefully. *How would it look if I let myself fall in love with the father of my—*

"I've been smelling roses all day," he said, "and it dawned on me just now that the wonderful aroma was coming from you!"

—students? she continued. *Especially when—*

"You looked very pretty today," he added. "If the parishioners held a contest, I'm sure you'd have won the prize for prettiest lady at the picnic."

For a fleeting moment, Valerie wished that she wasn't Freeland's only teacher, that he still hadn't gotten over the loss of his wife, and that she hadn't been hardened by the ruins of war....

She licked her lips, acknowledging that there were many other logical reasons why she shouldn't feel this way about him, especially considering she'd known him for such a short time. Gathering the basket and her skirts, she whispered, "I—I'd better go inside so you can get those poor, exhausted children into bed." She was nearly standing, ready to jump down from the buckboard, when he wrapped his big hand around her slender wrist.

"There's a church social next Saturday. Will you do me the honor of accompanying me, Miss Carter?"

She'd seen that look before on the faces of the boys in her class—when they missed an assignment, arrived late at school, or asked permission to leave early. It was the wide-eyed, innocent expression that pleaded for her approval, for her affirmative response.

This was proof, she thought, staring into his velvety brown eyes, of the inappropriateness of forming an attachment to him. She searched her mind for a polite yet firm way to say no. Not a single idea materialized, though, and she slumped back onto the wagon seat, hoping the action would pump blood into her brain and stimulate her idle imagination. "I'd like that," she said, surprising herself. "I'd like it very much, Mr. Collins."

"Good," he said, grinning as he gave her wrist a little squeeze. Then, he hopped down from the wagon and hurried around to her side and, after placing her basket beside a huge wooden wheel, held out his arms. At the church, when he'd gripped her waist to help her down, he'd released her the moment her feet had touched the ground. This time, he held on to her as his gaze fused to hers. "Now then, tell me what it'll take to get you to call me Paul...."

She hadn't realized until that moment just how cold and lonely her life had become, how alone she'd been. Oh, how good it felt, how *comforting*, to stand in the warm circle of his arms! "I'll call you Paul," she began, "if you'll call me Valerie." She hesitated. "But... need I remind you how many tongues we set to wagging today?"

"Most all of them, I reckon."

"Then, you'll agree, I'm sure, that for your children's sakes, as well as our own, we should reserve the familiar addresses for...." Valerie didn't want to presume too much. Or too soon. "...Only for those very rare occasions when we might find ourselves alone."

One eyebrow rose high on his forehead as he considered her words, then nodded, a lazy smile softening his features. "Ah, dear Valerie, I have a feeling it's going to be a very long week," he said as his face moved slowly, slowly closer.

Logic, reason, and the many arguments she'd outlined for keeping a careful distance from him vanished from her mind as she steadied herself for their first kiss. But when his lips finally made contact, it was with her cheek. She hid her disappointment behind a fake yawn.

"A mighty long week," he repeated, chuckling as he drew her into a light embrace.

Once the kids were tucked into bed, Paul sat in the rocker, staring blankly into the flickering fire, his Bible open on his lap. The bright, coppery flames reminded him of the way the sunlight glowed in Valerie's hair.

"What got into me today?" he prayed aloud. "I was acting like some fool youngster head over heels in love for the first time in his life."

And why not? he asked himself. He wasn't a grizzled old man. Yet. And Rita had been gone for nearly five years. The time had come to get back to the business of living life again—for the children's sakes, as well as his own.

He remembered the night not so long ago when he'd promised they'd do just that. They'd needed to hear the words every bit as much as he'd needed to say them, for every moment since had been brighter. Laughter filled the house once more, and no sad crying woke him in the dark of night. They'd taken him at his word; it *was* time to put the past behind them—the sad parts of it, anyway.

So, today, with Valerie, he'd tried to practice what he'd preached. He owed them that much. Owed it to himself, too.

Her laughter echoed in his mind. Her smile, serene and lovely, shone at him each time he closed his eyes. And those eyes, glowing with life and intelligence, glittered more brightly than any gem he'd ever seen. She wasn't afraid to ask questions, and she didn't fear answers, either. He'd watched her from afar, and up close, too, marveling that no matter whom she talked with, whether man or woman, infant or grandparent, she roused the same interested response.

He'd read about the Northern Lights that lit up the heavens like a miraculous glow; the same beauty was enjoyed by all viewers, whether in Canada, Iceland, or the Arctic. Valerie's personality was like that!

Her joy was contagious, inspiring everyone to seek her out. She didn't seem to mind in the least, even though, all through the day, children and adults alike demanded her attention, interrupted her conversations, and disturbed those rare moments of solitude she so obviously enjoyed.

Perhaps she was an angel, sent to the earth to dispense happiness and high-spiritedness, to dispel gloom and doom wherever she went. Her joy was all the more amazing for emanating from a woman who'd suffered many tragedies.

He'd noticed a most curious thing, though. When he'd said grace before their picnic meal, the "angel" hadn't folded her hands, bowed her head, or closed her eyes. When he'd finished the prayer, she hadn't said amen. It seemed strange, because he'd seen her in church every Sunday since moving to Freeland. Surely, she was a follower....

Of course, she's a follower! he rebuked himself. No one but a follower of Christ could be moved to tears by the sight of an eagle, as she had during their lunch, or stunned into awed silence by a sleeping infant, as she'd been when they'd first arrived at the churchyard. No one could have brought pure joy to so many unless the light of God was shining brightly within her.

She'd spent more than half of her first week's salary on supplies for the school. He'd overheard her say in the general store, "Education should teach equality first and foremost. How can we accomplish that if one child has a slate, and another has none, simply because one family can afford it and another can't?"

In just over a month, Miss Valerie Carter had earned a reputation for having a soft touch. No child's tears went unheeded. No student's needs went unmet. If a mother needed flour in order to prepare a healthy lunch for her child, it mysteriously appeared on her porch. If a father had no money to buy shoes for his son, making the long walk to school impossible, a pair of boots in exactly the right size appeared outside his door.

"Where would *I* get the money to do the work of old St. Nick?" Valerie would scoff when asked if she'd played a part in the little miracles.

But Paul had been in the store when she'd purchased a pair of tiny black boots. "What're these for?" Greta had wanted to know as Valerie counted out the coins that made them her boots—at least temporarily. "You got some tiny tootsies there, Miss Carter, but they ain't squeezin' into these here shoes!"

She'd blushed furiously, fumbling with her purse strings, and said, "I have a nephew in Richmond, you see, and his birthday is coming up...."

Paul had known immediately that she was fibbing, and he'd silently judged her, for all untruths, he believed, were unholy. But the very next day, when Emmet Saunders had stopped by to deliver the load of wood Paul had ordered, he'd said, "Strangest thing happened 'bout three days ago, when my boy come home whinin' 'cause his boots was too small. Still, off to the schoolhouse he went next mornin', where Miss Carter wrapped his blisters in bandages and told him not to worry, 'cause he'd get new shoes right soon. And don't y'know, the very next day, there's a pair o' shiny boots just his size out on the porch, an' the boy's callin' me a hero. Didn't have the heart to admit it, Paul, but I never bought 'em!"

The story had forced Paul to reevaluate his rigid opinion about tall tales. Seeing how the "miracle" had affected Emmet and his family had taught Paul that the good Valerie had done outweighed the slight fib she'd told. And she'd done the deed without embarrassing Emmet and his family.

Yes, God lived in her, all right. And he'd see to it she started admitting it, by golly!

Chapter Four

It was harvest time, and Valerie hadn't seen any Freeland farmers—or many of their children—in weeks. The town earned its reputation for producing the best corn and wheat in the state, but doing so required long, hard days in the fields. Though she'd lived through harvests at Carter Hall, she'd never missed school because of them. But these after-war times were hard, and some of her students, the older boys in particular, were needed at home.

She learned the meaning of the phrase "burning the midnight oil," for it took her hours to produce an abbreviated version of the day's schoolwork for the farm boys, who'd be too exhausted after a hard day's work to complete a full lesson. But no sacrifice was too great for the sake of her students.

Most lessons were delivered to absent students by brothers, sisters, or neighbors. Children without siblings, or those who lived too far away to get their work from friends, found themselves face-to-face with their pretty young teacher no less than once a week. And, since acres and miles separated the farms, Valerie was often forced to make her deliveries at suppertime. As often as not, the lady of the house would insist that Valerie join the family for a tasty, hot meal. Halfway through the harvest season, she'd helped wash so many supper plates and cups that her hands were growing dry and red.

If Valerie did more than was expected for her pupils, she went far past the call of duties for their families. She'd shown Otto and Helga Kratt's mother how to add and subtract, explained the Boston Tea Party to Gregg Pratt's mom, loaned Katrina Albert's mother her collection of Shakespeare's works, and even taught Frank Calvert's mother to read and write. Though Valerie swore them all to secrecy, the whole town was talking about how God had blessed them the day Valerie Carter had decided to make Freeland, Maryland, her home.

Paul Collins, in particular, knew how lucky they were to have Valerie in their lives, for she gave his motherless children special, individual attention—and she did it so matter-of-factly that they never felt any different from youngsters with two parents.

When the harvest ended, Paul began delivering lunch to his children again, and, if the weather allowed, the Collins family would munch their meal together under the big maple in the school yard. Though he never missed a word from his children's mouths, his seat facing the window-wall of the schoolhouse allowed him to watch as Valerie erased the morning's lesson from the big blackboard and replaced it with another, stacked books on the shelves, and rearranged the desks in neat, straight rows.

In church, deliberately choosing a pew across the aisle and a few rows back enabled him to see Valerie during Sunday services. He knew that she shopped in the general store very early on Saturday mornings, so he adjusted his regular shopping day and time accordingly. More often than he cared to admit, he found himself daydreaming, and Miss Valerie Carter was always the subject of his musings. Fumbling for excuses to talk with her, Paul believed his conversations swung from the mundane to the ridiculous: weather, fences that needed repairing, a pesky, loose board on his front porch....

Never in his life had he been so unfocused. Never had he been so easily distracted. He buried his nose in his Bible every evening, praying that the Lord would show him why he thought of Valerie first thing every morning; why she came to mind so many times each day; why, oh why, he pictured her sweet smile and heard her musical voice sing in his memory the last thing every night. He thanked the Lord that no one else had noticed.

Or so he thought....

At breakfast one Saturday morning, Timmy asked, "Pa, why do you stare at Miss Carter all the time?"

He'd been sopping gravy with his biscuit and nearly dropped the bread in his lap. "I don't stare," Paul said, his voice cracking with defensive frustration.

"Not *all* the time, anyway," Tyler teased. "Only when he's awake...."

To hide his flush of embarrassment, Paul reached for the milk pitcher, though his glass was nearly full.

Tricia giggled as he topped it off. "Maybe you're in love, Pa."

Tyler groaned. "Pa...say it ain't so!"

"Papa loves Miss Carter," Timmy said in singsong, "Papa loves Miss Carter...."

"Timmy! Enough of that nonsense!" Paul thundered. "You've put off gathering those eggs long enough. Now get busy!" Facing Tyler, he narrowed his eyes. "Have you stacked that firewood yet like I told you to? And Tricia, did you mend that shirt I brought you yesterday?"

Quietly, the children shuffled off to do their chores. He heard their giggles, muffled by hands over their mouths, and as the kitchen door was shut, he couldn't suppress a smile of his own. But as hard as he tried to ignore it, Timmy's question gonged in his mind for the rest of the day. Why *did* he stare at Valerie all the time?

When she'd first come to Freeland, he'd overheard talk in town. "Spoiled little rich girl," folks had called her. Not many had expected her to be much of a teacher. Not many had expected she'd be much of anything, in fact. But talk these days was more along the lines of, "How'd we ever get along without her?"

She'd singlehandedly whipped the ramshackle little house behind the school into shape, wielding hammer and sawing wood as well as any man. She didn't complain, like other women, when sugar was in short supply, or when they were out of lace at the general store. If anyone needed her for anything, she was there, lickety-split. No wonder Freelanders respected and admired her. No wonder they loved Valerie Carter.

But did *he*?

Paul decided he'd better give the question a good deal of thought...and a whole lot of prayer.

Early one gray October morning, as DeWitt Frank swept the steps of his general store, his wife's high-pitched hollering disturbed his tranquil mood. "Have mercy," Greta shouted, holding her nose and pointing at the raggedy dog that had trotted onto the porch. "Shoo dat mutt away. He schtinks to high heaven!"

DeWitt swished his broom in the canine's direction. "Go 'vay," he ordered it. "Go, now. Scoot! Ve don't need der likes o' you schmellin' up der store!"

The dog sat on its haunches, cocked its head, and whimpered pathetically.

"Vhat're you vaitink for?" Greta demanded. "Git him gone before he scares away our customers!"

DeWitt was about to bop the pup with his broom when Valerie rounded the corner.

"Don't!"

Paul, who'd just finished shopping in the store, hefted a fifty-pound bag of flour onto the buckboard, then folded his arms over his chest and stood back to watch the scene unfold.

"He's gotta go, Miss Carter," DeWitt explained. "Ve don't know vere he's been...."

"Und ve doessn't care," Greta interrupted him. "He can't schtay here schmellin' like dat! Schmack him, DeVitt! Go on, giff him a goot one, right on der rump!"

Valerie, unmindful of its filthy fur, wrapped the terrified dog in a protective hug. "What's the matter, boy?" she crooned. "Is everybody picking on you?" She shot an angry glare at Greta. "There's absolutely no need to beat the poor creature."

Greta scowled. "Fine, den," the gray-haired old woman snapped. "You take responsibility for da ugly beast. Zee if I care. But if he bites you, don't come cryin' to me!" she added before stomping into the store and slamming the door behind her.

Valerie opened her mouth to defend the dog to DeWitt. "Don't look at me," Greta's husband said, his hands raised in mock surrender. "I chust vork here." With that, he, too, disappeared into the store.

"Well, looks like it's just you and me, boy," Valerie whispered to the dog. She sat down on the top step of the porch to evaluate her new friend. "Burrs and mud...and I'll bet you have a whole colony of fleas living on you, too," she said, scratching his chin.

Suddenly, she stood up and ran toward the street. Patting her thighs, Valerie called, "C'mon, boy! Wanna play follow the leader?"

Its eyes bright and ears perked up, the dog stood on all fours, then bounded down the street behind the sure-footed little woman.

Grinning, Paul shook his head. As much as he would have liked to see how things turned out for the dirty mutt, he had no time for such shenanigans today. He had business at the bank, the blacksmith's, and the feed and grain store. Paul climbed onto the wagon's padded seat and whistled his horse to attention.

As he headed for his next stop, he grinned, aware that no other woman would have defended the mangy mutt. No other woman would have weathered Greta's wrath to save its sorry hide. And, he acknowledged with a chuckle, no other woman would run through the center of town with a stray dog yipping happily at her heels.

An hour later, when he walked around to the back of her house, she was soaked from head to toe. The dog, standing in a steaming tub of clear water, actually seemed to be enjoying its bath. "You look better already," he heard her say. "I might just keep you once I get you all cleaned up. What do you think of that?"

"I think he'd be a fool not to love the idea."

He'd startled her. Paul could see that much in her wide, green eyes.

"Sakes alive," she said. "You must be part cat—I didn't even hear you coming."

Laughter rumbled deep in his chest, but Paul swallowed it. "This is quite an undertaking. You sure you're up to it?"

Valerie brushed her damp bangs from her forehead, the back of her hand leaving a trail of bubbles on her pale, smooth skin. "He's a dog," she pointed out, "not a Bengal tiger. I realize menfolk don't put much stock in a woman's ability to do things for herself, but I think I can handle—"

"I never meant to imply you couldn't handle it," he interrupted her. "I just wondered if you'd given any thought to how much work he'll be."

Valerie sighed. Dipping a soup ladle into the tub of clear water, she began rinsing suds from the dog's back. "Work?" She grinned, blowing bubbles from her upper lip. "You call this work? Why, I'm having the time of my life!"

Paul laughed. If it had been anyone else covered with suds, he might have disagreed. He grabbed one of the towels Valerie had stacked on the small wooden stool beside the tub and draped it around his neck. Then, hoisting the dog from the water, he fluffed its fur. The mutt, glad to be on dry ground again, shook out as Paul squinted to protect his eyes from the water droplets flying every which way.

"Oh, dear," Valerie said, smiling as she filled the ladle with water, "you're all wet." With no warning, she added, "But not nearly wet enough." And then she doused him.

Her childlike glee was contagious. "So, you like to play rough, do you?" he asked, picking up the half-filled tub of sudsy water. "Let's see just how rough you like it!"

Squealing like a schoolgirl, she dodged left and right, holding her skirts slightly up in front of her, running in circles and hiding behind trees until he finally got his vengeance.

"You look like a drowned rat," he said, his hearty laughter bouncing all around her yard.

"I feel like one, too," Valerie admitted, blinking as water dripped from her soaked hair into her eyes. Then she sneezed. And sneezed again.

A feeling of fierce protectiveness swelled within him. Immediately, Paul wrapped her tightly in the second towel and draped his arm around her shoulders. "We'd better get you inside where it's warm before you catch your death of cold," he said, leading her toward the house.

The pooch, padding along happily beside them, seemed to take for granted that he was home, that Valerie was his mistress now. The minute his paws crossed the threshold, he lay down in front of the woodstove as if he'd been doing it since he was a pup.

Paul took a thick quilt from the back of a chair and bundled Valerie into it. Next, he built a roaring fire in the potbelly stove, filled the teapot with water from the kitchen pump, and proceeded to brew her a cup of strong, hot tea.

Valerie was still shivering after she downed the first cup.

"Stand up," he said, taking her hands in his own. "Let's get the blood moving in those puny arms of yours." Vigorously, he rubbed her upper arms. He'd expected her to fuss and refuse his help. Instead, she complied without a word of complaint. She looked tiny and vulnerable, facing him in her small kitchen. She'd always seemed brave and forceful, strong and capable. But the way she stood now, surprisingly quiet and shy as he rubbed her shoulders, made him realize she had a fragile, delicate side, as well. Impulsively, he pulled her into a hug and tenderly pressed her cheek to his chest. It felt good to have her in his arms—so good, in fact, that Paul decided it must be where she belonged. At least, this was where he wanted her to be.

All through the night, Valerie thought about that tiny fragment in time when she'd stood, wrapped in Paul's warm embrace. It had seemed impossible at the time, but she could have sworn that he'd trembled. Surely, it had been no more than a reaction to the coldness of his damp clothes....

He'd stoked the fire and fixed her one last cup of tea, and, after making her promise to eat the leftover soup and biscuits he'd found on the stovetop, he'd left.

And Valerie knew she'd see that wide, handsome smile in her dreams.

The dog refused to leave her side, even for a moment, and Valerie quickly discovered she rather liked having a furry shadow. She shared her supper with him, then settled down in front of the fire, her new pal snuggling against her feet. "Tomorrow, we're going to find something to call you. You're a scruffy old thing, but you deserve a proper name."

After a moment, she said, "Wait—that's it! I'll call you Scruffy!"

The dog woofed, as if in agreement, and rested his head on her knees.

Valerie blew out the lantern flame and climbed into bed. "G'night, Scruffy," she whispered into the darkness, then drifted off to sleep.

She dreamed she'd been walking in the woods and a tree had fallen on her legs, pinning her to the mossy earth. Tossing and turning, Valerie struggled to wriggle from beneath the broad trunk. Would she be permanently paralyzed? A powerful ache in her thighs woke her as the first rays of sunlight peeked through the shuttered window. It took a moment to put the dream together with reality. "Scruffy, you big lummox," she half scolded, laughing, "move over! You've cut off all circulation in my legs!"

Yawning sleepily, the dog obliged. Valerie rubbed her legs vigorously to get the blood flowing in them again.

The act reminded her of the way Paul had rubbed her shoulders the night before. The dream of the fallen tree was immediately forgotten, for she preferred to remember other, sweeter dreams she'd had during the night—dreams of quiet chats over picnic lunches, long buggy rides on sultry summer evenings, playful games of water tag on crisp, fall afternoons, and the happiness that exists between a perfectly matched pair.

What are you thinking? she suddenly admonished herself. *He's hardly the ideal mate for you...or you for him!* She did admire most everything about him, from his loyalty to the children to his dedication to the farm. He was smart, sweet, and funny, too...when he chose to let his guard down. His only flaw, as she saw it, was his doggedly determined devotion to God.

Didn't Paul realize that even without God, things would be exactly the same? Hadn't he ever asked himself why, if his God was so all-fired powerful, He hadn't spared Paul's wife and her unborn baby? Couldn't he see that prayer didn't change anything, or that no amount of faith would alter life's course?

Valerie had been a follower once. But that was long ago, when she'd been young and naïve. She'd grown up since then. Grown up a lot. Time had taught her that blind belief is a dangerous thing, for it gives one hope; and hope, she believed, would only disappoint you in the end.

Yes, she'd been one of the faithful, and when civil war had looked probable, she'd prayed it wouldn't happen. When it did, she'd prayed that the men in charge would do whatever they could to put an immediate stop to it. Of course, they hadn't, so she'd prayed that no one would be hurt. But the war hurt everyone, it seemed, in one way or another. It was a rare day when a friend or neighbor wasn't mourning a loved one killed in some horrible, bloody battle.

The war had destroyed her father's business, and then he'd been gunned down for harboring helpless, hungry slaves. Regardless of their ages, those who'd lost their lives in the War Between the States were husbands and fathers, sons and brothers. Her faith and prayers hadn't convinced God to protect her father or her brothers, or to protect her mother from grieving herself into an early grave.

While she'd still had the plantation, Valerie had prayed for the strength to run it in the way her father would have wanted. But the smoke and flames that had greedily devoured Carter Hall had been visible for miles after the Yankees had passed through...and God hadn't helped her douse them.

She believed God hadn't answered her prayers because He hadn't heard them.

Standing in the ashes of the only home she'd ever known, she'd realized there was one thing, and one thing only, that she could believe in: herself.

Yes, standing in the protective circle of Paul's arms had felt wonderful, but how could she put her trust in a man who blindly followed a Being who allowed such suffering and misery?

On the night she'd rescued Scruffy, she'd admitted to herself that she was falling in love with Paul Collins. But she'd also loved her father, brothers, and mother—all God-fearing people—and look where their blind faith had gotten them! Valerie couldn't bear to love and lose again. It was as simple as that.

Paul didn't understand Valerie's suddenly evasive behavior. If she saw him on the street, she crossed to the other side. If she realized he was in the same shop, she'd leave her goods on the counter and dash away like a scared rabbit. She must have sensed that he'd chosen a church pew with a clear view of her, for she began arriving late so that she could sit out of sight, way in the back. Though she'd agreed weeks before to meet him at a church social, she'd never showed up for it. And though she'd always been one to meet fears and confrontations head-on, she now avoided his eyes.

He missed her bright smile. Her teasing winks. Her silly jokes and her delightfully playful laughter. "Maybe you're in love," Tricia had said. And that was the simple truth. The proof was the big, gaping hole her absence made in his heart.

Paul prayed about it nearly as much as he thought about it— admittedly, a considerable investment of time.

Late one chilly October night, when the children had been tucked safely in bed, he held his Bible to his breast and closed his eyes. "Dear God," he prayed, "help me understand what this lesson will teach me."

Suddenly, the quilt Rita had made, stitch by stitch, slipped from his lap onto the floor. Paul gathered it up and folded it neatly before hanging it over the arm of his chair. Stroking its soft, colorful squares, he remembered happy times with his wife. He hadn't thought of her nearly as often, nor missed her nearly as much, as he had before meeting Valerie. A stab of guilt cut through him. How could he so coldly and willingly set aside her memory? How could he so callously blot her from his mind? The answer was simple: He'd put Rita's death out of his mind because Valerie reminded him how much he'd missed *living*.

Valerie had taught his children to live again, too. Taught them that it was all right, even respectable, to laugh and play and enjoy life, even though their mother was gone. "Nobody expects you to forget your ma," he heard her telling them one day when he surprised them at the schoolhouse, "but if she knew the three of you were sad-eyed all the time, it would just break her heart."

Paul suspected the children missed their extra time with Valerie as much as he did. Once a week, at least, she'd stopped by the farm, her wicker picnic basket overflowing with cookies, sourdough bread, a hot-from-the-oven fruit pie, or vegetables she'd grown and simmered into delicious soups and stews.

And books...oh, how she could make a story come to life Paul had loved listening as she read to his children, for Valerie's zest for life wasn't just evident in her lyrical voice—it was contagious.

He'd never thought he'd love again. At least, he'd never thought it was possible to love like *that* twice in one lifetime. But just as Valerie had proved him wrong about putting Rita's memory in its proper place, she was proving him wrong about the human heart's capacity to love....

Grinning, Paul slapped his knee. *That's it!* he decided. He'd been feeling guilty for wanting to move forward with Valerie—it seemed a betrayal of his love for Rita. In truth, he recognized, it was the pure, sweet love he'd felt for his wife that made him yearn for that special kind of closeness again.

His Bible fell open to Psalm 107:6: "*They cried unto the* LORD *in their trouble, and he delivered them out of their distresses.*" It was as plain as the book in his lap: God had heard his cries, and Valerie was the answer to his prayers.

He closed the Good Book and placed it gently on the mantle. "Just one problem left to solve, Lord," he whispered, his smile fading slightly as he stroked the Bible's black leather binding. "How do I get Valerie back again when I don't know how I lost her in the first place?"

Chapter Five

As she descended the wide plank steps of the church, Valerie managed to nod politely in response to the good mornings and howdy-dos of fellow Freelanders. Was Paul Collins to blame for her confused, distracted state of mind? Valerie couldn't be sure....

She told herself it only *seemed* that he'd stared at her all during the service, and that he hadn't *really* been grinning and winking and wiggling his eyebrows at her. He was far too devout a Christian to misbehave like an unruly schoolboy, especially right in the middle of the pastor's sermon about giving the Lord nothing less than one's best!

Her father's old saying gonged in her mind: "Facts are facts!" Either Paul had been making eyes at her all through the Sunday service or she was losing her mind.

Walking along the redbrick path that led from the church steps to the road, Valerie smiled and placed a white-gloved hand over her fluttering heart. Facts were facts, all right. Paul Collins had been flirting with her from his aisle seat, right there in front of his children and the entire congregation. She'd nearly reached the end of the fence that surrounded the churchyard when the *clickety-clack* of tree twig against pickets made her realize that, at some point during her short walk, she'd picked up a small, fallen branch.

Flushing slightly at her own silliness, Valerie dropped the stick. Suddenly, the giddy, girlish response to his grins and winks disappeared, and, in its place, the list of his positive attributes grew. He was tall, handsome, hardworking, responsible…decent and good, too…and a wonderful, loving father…. He deserved a woman who would share his life—every aspect of it, down to and including his love for the Lord. And Valerie could not—*would* not—blindly follow the One responsible for her solitary status in the world.

She found herself standing at her gate, staring blankly at the front of her cottage. *How did I get this far without realizing it?* she wondered. *You're acting like a moon-struck schoolgirl who's never been in love before!* As she shoved the gate open and stomped up her narrow, cobbled walk, Valerie admitted that she *hadn't* been in love before. At least, she'd never experienced anything quite as intense as this….

Lately, as she'd corrected homework papers, Valerie had needed to forcibly blink Paul's charming grin from her memory. And just the other day, amid the *whisk-whisk* sounds of her sweeping, she'd found herself leaning on the broom handle and grinning like a simpleton, remembering the way he'd drenched her with Scruffy's rinsewater. Now, as she entered her dim, quiet kitchen, she had to admit that if she hadn't tilted her own head to get a better view of him during the church service that day, she wouldn't have known that he'd been watching her.

She listened for the reassuring *click* that told her the big oak door had shut out the rest of the world. Safe in her own little domain, she leaned against the door and took a deep, cleansing breath. *Get ahold of yourself. You know better than to get involved with a man like that,* she told herself.

But…a man like *what?*

If she had a mind to settle down with one man for the rest of her life, she could do far worse than the likes of Paul Collins—that much she knew. A future with a man like that would be filled with peace and contentment, joy and laughter. No, he would never be able to give her a mansion or buy her a gilded carriage, but he'd make sure they had a roof over their heads—one that never leaked. He'd see to it that his children never wore rags or limped around in too-small boots, even if it meant working round the clock to buy what they needed. His family would never go hungry. Would never be cold. And his supply of warm embraces and reassuring words would be never-ending. A man like that....

Valerie took another deep breath. The mantle clock told her she'd been daydreaming about him for five minutes straight. Clearing her throat, Valerie slipped off her gloves, one finger at a time. Then, with a flick of her wrist, she untied the blue satin bonnet bow beneath her chin and headed for her bedroom. It wasn't until she slid open her bureau drawer to put away her gloves that she saw the picture that always brought tears to her eyes.

She took off her bonnet, picked up the heavy brass picture frame, and blinked at the frozen images of her family, captured forever in hazy brown. Her father and mother, stern in their stiff-collared clothes and plastered-down hair, were standing side by side behind their three children. Valerie, a mere ten years old at the time, was sitting between her brothers, Lee Junior and Delbert, whose lopsided grins told everyone who viewed the aging photo-graph that they were proud of the couple with their hands clamped protectively on their sons' shoulders.

Slowly, Valerie carried the picture into the parlor, sat down in her cushioned rocker, and let the tears roll freely down her cheeks. She couldn't remember the last time she'd really cried over her family. For a few moments, she couldn't figure out why a few innocent winks from Paul Collins would remind her of how much she missed them.

When the realization set in, she hugged the photograph to her breast and sobbed uncontrollably. She'd always had an independent spirit. It had gotten her into trouble often as a child, for it had spurred her to investigating places and things and creatures that "could be dangerous," as her mother would often warn. She'd never been a clingy girl, preferring to walk along Richmond's busy streets on her own rather than remain connected hand in hand to either of her parents. But that independent spirit had never led her far from home or hearth; even as a youngster, Valerie had sensed that love, protection, and everything else she'd ever need would come by way of those two sturdy, dependable people.

She cried because she missed them...and because she missed being part of a loving family.

A man like that....

Memories of chatting with her father by the fireside, helping her mother decorate the house for Christmas, and gathering willow branches and turning them into fishing poles with her brothers filled her mind. She remembered carriage rides into town. Moonlit walks. Playing hide-and-seek with her brothers. Valerie didn't just miss her family. She missed family *life*, and it had been Paul who'd reminded her that she was completely and utterly alone in the world.

And why was she so totally alone? Because his precious *God* had turned a deaf ear to her and, one by one, had taken from her all those she held dear.

She stood up quickly and headed to her bedroom, where she gently placed the photograph on her dresser before marching to the kitchen to prepare herself a midday meal. She'd have cold, thinly sliced roast beef with bread and butter pickles on the side, along with a slice of the sourdough bread she'd baked the night before. And she'd wash it all down with a cup of strong, hot tea.

Valerie put a lot of effort into her meals. Somehow, setting a proper table made eating alone seem a little less bleak. So, as she waited for the water to boil, she smoothed the white linen table-cloth and put a silver knife and spoon to the right of the rose-patterned plate, a matching fork to its left. The cup and saucer, she placed just to the right of the knife's tip. She folded a soft napkin into a neat rectangle and placed it in the center of the dish as fresh tears welled in her eyes.

Valerie dropped into her chair and buried her face in her hands. It wasn't like her to give in to self-pity. What had gotten into her?

She blamed the bright, sunny day. Then the crisp, autumn breeze. The pastor's long-winded sermon. The children's angelic voices singing "Amazing Grace."

But it was the photograph, she knew, that had stirred her long-resting emotions. Angrily, she admitted she'd still be surrounded by the loving people in the photograph if Paul's all-wonderful God had only answered her prayers!

Were my prayers that unreasonable? she ranted silently, staring at the tin kitchen ceiling. *You parted the seas, turned water into wine…. You had the power to save them! Why didn't You save them?*

It had been over a year since she'd buried the last of her family, and she'd thought that the worst of her grieving had ended. She'd cried bitterly at their funerals, cried angrily at their gravesites. In time, the tears had come less often and with less intensity. She'd been in Freeland for months now and hadn't had reason to shed a single tear. *So why,* she asked herself, *are you weeping uncontrollably now?*

Tears, in her mind, were a symptom of inner weakness. And weakness made her angry. She could abide sadness and tears in others, especially in children. But not in herself. Tears of anger were the worst kind of all, for they were rooted in self-pity. And self-pity, her father had taught her, was the single most destructive human character trait.

With calm deliberateness, she took the teapot off the flame, wrapped the roast beef in oilcloth, and slid the bread into the wooden breadbox. Once the pickles were back in their Mason jar, she rinsed the bowl they'd been in. Then, after brushing crumbs from the bread plate, she put the lovely dishes back into the cupboard and returned the tablecloth and napkin to the sideboard drawer. She knew better than to cherish these material possessions, for she'd seen how quickly and cruelly things could be snatched away. But these few pieces of china, the beautiful white linen tablecloth, and the three matching napkins were almost the only things she'd managed to salvage from the fire that destroyed Carter Hall. These, and the photograph....

She untied her red gingham apron and hung it on the peg beside the door, then headed for her bedroom. When she came out again, she was wearing old boots and a threadbare dress. Her thick, dark hair, fastened with a ribbon atop her head in a ponytail, was mostly hidden by a wide-brimmed straw hat.

Scruffy was sitting on the porch when Valerie stepped outside. "Well, how long have you been back?" she asked the dog. "You were nowhere to be seen when I got back from church." She squatted to ruffle his sandy-colored fur. "You haven't been up to no good, now, have you?"

Scruffy licked Valerie's cheek and gave a breathy bark.

"Try to stay close to home," she said as she headed for the shed out back. "I don't want to be hollering for you like some fishwife come dark...."

She'd get her vegetable garden cleaned up this afternoon if it was the last thing she'd do. Taking her work gloves from the high shelf just inside the shed, she scanned the semidark space in search of her spade. Just as she reached out to grab it, a horrible, high-pitched scream made her blood run cold.

Though Valerie's house was tucked snugly out of sight behind the school, it sat in the hub of Freeland. The Northern Central Railroad tracks paralleled Main Street, and every store along the road was within walking distance. At times such as this, while running in the direction of the frightening scream, Valerie almost wished she lived high on a hill, out of earshot of the town's bustling activities.

"What is it?" she asked, breathless from her run.

Greta, her face half hidden behind one of her large, calloused hands, dabbed her blue eyes with a lace-trimmed handkerchief. "I found diss tacked to my door chust now," she cried. "Dose men who killed Yonson, it iss from dem."

"Johnson?" Valerie pictured the ever smiling face of the town blacksmith, Abel Johnson. "Abel Johnson is dead? But how...?"

Greta swallowed a sob. "Dey hanged him. Dey vas here in der middle of der night," she explained tearfully.

Valerie took the note from Greta's trembling hands and read silently: "*If you want to keep living in this town,*" said the precisely lettered threat, "*you'll forget everything you saw.*"

Valerie's heartbeat quickened. "Greta," she whispered, "what exactly did you see?"

The older woman sniffed loudly. "Dose men. Riding on big horses, wearing white robes...." Her blue eyes darted back and forth as she scanned the street for possible eavesdroppers before casting a sidelong glance in Valerie's direction. "You vouldn't tell anybody...?"

Valerie shook her head. "Of course not. I'd never put you and DeWitt in jeopardy, but—"

"—but notink! Surely, you've heard of the Vite Bruderhood!"

Valerie nodded. She'd heard of them, all right. They were a savage pack of men who hid their identities beneath white hoods and robes. According to an article in the *Gazette*, the secret society, which had begun organizing its members almost as soon as the Civil War ended, had stayed deep in the South, near Pulaski, Tennessee, its town of origin. They called themselves the Ku Klux Klan. The Pale Faces. The Constitutional Union Guards. The Order of the White Rose. Whatever name they went by, they'd taken it upon themselves to continue the tradition of slavery, despite the fact that so many men had given their lives to put an end to the ugly institution. The Klan firmly believed in white supremacy and believed just as firmly in their right to do whatever they deemed necessary to protect the purity of their race.

"I vas never so afraid in all my life," Greta sighed. "Dey vas terrible to look at."

Valerie led the trembling older woman up the steps and into the quiet seclusion of her feed and grain store. "Let me fix you a cup of tea," Valerie offered, puttering in the tiny kitchen behind the curtained storefront.

Greta sagged into the seat of a straight-backed wooden chair and rested her elbows on the table. Holding her head in her hands, she said, "Dey vould haff been scary enough in dose pointed hats wit' dose big eye holes cut into dem. But dey had skulls on dere saddle horns, too!"

According to the *Gazette* article, the white-robed uniforms and saddle skulls represented the spirits of dead Rebel soldiers. Valerie pictured the gang on horseback, all wearing the dreadful costumes. Even in the bold light of day, they would have been terrifying. She could only imagine how frightening the scene might be, shrouded in darkness.

"Und da torches. Huge, bright fire sticks dat lit up der sky. Ve never even heard dem coming," Greta continued, "'cause dey had wrapped da horses' hooves wit' blankets. Suddenly, dey vas everywhere. All 'round Yonson's shop und up und down der street."

Valerie had always slept deeply. She remembered wishing her house were far above the melee of town sounds, as she'd run toward the sounds of Greta's screams. Now, she altered her wish. If she'd heard something, perhaps she could have gone for help. Perhaps she could have done something to stop the Klan before—

"Dey beat him wit' sticks und clubs," Greta was saying. "Und when he fell to de ground, dey kicked him, over und over. He vasn't even conscious when dey put dat rope around hiss neck…."

Telling that part of the story upset Greta more than anything else she'd said so far. Valerie sensed that if the woman kept what she'd seen to herself, she would see it for the rest of her life every time she closed her eyes. "Don't keep their dirty secret," Valerie urged her. "Talk about it. Tell me. Tell everyone you know!"

She put a mug of steaming tea down in front of Greta, then patted a chubby, work-hardened hand. But Greta's stony, tight-lipped expression made it clear that she had no intention of saying another word.

"It just amazes me how men can be so pigheaded," Valerie said. "This country isn't even a hundred years old yet, and already they seem to have forgotten why it was established in the first place!"

Greta took a slow sip of her tea, then met Valerie's gaze. "Dey mean vhat dey say," she whispered. "I should not haff told you vhat I saw. Now you could be in danger, too. Good ting DeVitt iss busy out back. He vould be furious witt me if he knew I told you…."

Gritting her teeth, Valerie sat down across from Greta. "It's wrong to keep quiet about what happened. You should tell the sheriff what you saw. Because if you don't, Abel Johnson won't be the only Negro man to die at the Klan's hands."

Greta sat, wide-eyed and open-mouthed, staring at Valerie. After a long silence, she said softly, "Dat may be true enough. But I cannot risk it." She sandwiched Valerie's hands between her own. "Please don't make me sorry dat I spoke to you as a friend, Valerie. Tell me you'll keep my secret."

"But what about Abel's family?" Valerie pressed. "Don't you think they'd like to know the truth?"

Greta's tear-rasped voice cracked. "Dey vere dere. Dey saw de same t'ing dat I saw."

Against her better judgment, Valerie nodded her assent. She had to respect the old woman's fear, even if she didn't understand it.

"Vill you pray for me und DeVitt?" Greta asked, her voice quaking with emotion.

Valerie wanted to tell her friend the absolute truth—that the last thing in the world she'd do was pray for their safety. She'd seen the futility of prayer too many times. But, knowing that some folks drew strength from it, Valerie nodded, deciding not to shake Greta's already tentative hold on faith. She rose and headed for the door. "You're sure you don't want me to get the sheriff?"

"I chust vant to forget vhat happened to Yonson."

"If only we could...."

Tomorrow, like the rest of the folks in town, she'd watch as Abel's wife and three small children joined his parents and siblings in the funeral march down Main Street.

No, they would not forget.... "Well, I'll be here if you need to talk."

Getting home meant crossing the street and walking past Abel Johnson's blacksmith shop. Chills ran up and down Valerie's spine as she neared the giant oak where Greta said they'd killed him.

As she got closer, she saw the hemp rope, its ragged end swinging lazily in the breeze, that had been the Klan's murder weapon.

Valerie fumed. Keeping quiet about such madness, such violence, would only encourage those horrible men to commit similar crimes. A secret like Greta's would only give them courage to strike again and again, knowing that their frightening power could silence even the strongest-willed citizens, like Greta and DeWitt. Such silence guaranteed the Klan's return.

Valerie had been born and raised in Richmond, and her Southern pride flowed in her veins, pumped in her heart, echoed in her head. She'd lost everything to the horrible War Between the States and had witnessed the slaughter of humans, livestock, and pets at the hands of the Yankees. But even she understood the difference between the ravages of war and the senseless brutalization of innocent, hardworking Americans.

Today, the Johnson family would mourn their beloved Abel.

Valerie couldn't help but wonder which family would mourn a family member tomorrow.

Chapter Six

All too soon, Old Man Winter would blow frigid winds across the land and blanket Abel Johnson's grave with pure, white snow.

Until now, Valerie had passed her cousin Sally's house often, wishing that she and her family were home from their European holiday. She was glad now that Sally hadn't been in Freeland at the time of the grisly event.

Few townsfolk risked talking about the night Abel died, since no one could be sure that a friend, neighbor, or relative hadn't been one of those who'd donned the awful masks and robes to hang him. Ardith Johnson, unable to hire anyone to run the blacksmith shop, had been forced to sell it—and everything in it—for half of its true worth. The Johnsons had lived in the comfortable yet humble rooms behind the shop. Before Abel's murder, Ardith had browsed and bought things from the dress shop, the feed and grain, the hattery. Now, to make ends meet, she and her three young children lived on the drafty top floor of the Freelander Hotel. "I always been a dandy cook," she confided in Valerie one dreary rainy afternoon, "but who'da thought I'd be doing it for money someday?"

Ardith was a lovely young woman who worked long, hard hours without ever missing a Sunday service or a meeting at the schoolhouse. Yes, life was hard, the spunky lady admitted. "But we're all healthy. We got a roof over our heads an' plenty o' food in our bellies. The good Lord saw to it we'd be taken care of when He took sweet Abel home to Him."

The good Lord, indeed! Valerie fumed silently. *Why should those darling children and that wonderful woman have to live without Abel? Where was the good Lord when those murdering madmen tore through town, terrifying and killing an innocent citizen just because of his skin color?*

Valerie had said just that to Greta one day while waiting for the old woman to box up her grocery order. And Paul Collins had overheard every word of Valerie's rampage.

"'O ye of little faith,'" he said softly, interrupting her tirade.

She was growing a bit tired of his self-righteousness. How dare he quote Scripture to her simply because he presumed her to be faithless?

"Matthew chapter six, verse thirty," Valerie responded without hesitation.

Surprised at her immediate recognition of the age-old verse, Paul grinned. "'Watch ye, stand fast in the faith, quit you like men, be strong.'"

"First Corinthians chapter sixteen, verse thirteen. Believe it or not, Mr. Collins, I was raised in a strict Christian household. I know the Bible quite well," she snapped.

Confused by the fury of her response, Paul stopped grinning. "I'll concede that you've suffered many tragedies, Miss Carter," he said, assuming her uppity tone, "but the Lord isn't to blame for—"

"Then perhaps you'll be so kind as to tell me who *is* to blame," she interrupted him.

Without a word, he placed a hand on her elbow and guided her from the store to the school yard, where they sat on a narrow wooden bench beneath a weeping willow.

"Why I let you lead me here, I'll never know," she said, looking straight ahead and primly folding her hands in her lap.

"You followed because you're hoping I can provide you with the answers you're seeking. You're hurt and confused by your many personal losses. And in your loneliness, you want a place for that anger. You want someone to blame, and you've chosen the Lord."

Valerie stared down at her hands, unable to meet his eyes. She suspected that they would hold the same warmth and kindness she heard in his soft voice. And at the moment, she preferred to deal with facts, not emotions. "Greta told me that your father was a minister, and that you studied to be one, too," she began. "I'm sure you understand the grief and emptiness and anger one can feel when exposed to many losses. But please don't presume to understand why I feel as I do about God. You could never understand."

"Why not?" was his quiet question.

Valerie met his dark eyes. "Because you're a good man. Too good, in some ways."

That statement inspired a soft chuckle from him.

"Don't laugh at me, Paul. I'm serious."

His smile diminished. "I wasn't laughing at you, Valerie. I was laughing at the notion that I'm too good."

Ignoring his denial of her comment, she dropped her voice to a near whisper and said, "Others have lived harder lives than I, yet they continue to believe. To trust and have faith. Why? Because they're *good*. You're like that, Paul. You've suffered losses—hard and painful ones. Yet you've never doubted God's power. Your faith in Christ never faltered."

He took a deep breath and shook his head. "You're dead wrong on that score," he said after a moment. Before she could argue the point, he silenced her by going on to explain. "After I buried Rita,

I was angry. Furious, in fact. Inwardly, I ranted and raved because I'd prayed myself hoarse, yet the suffering and pain of those I loved seemed to go on and on." He began counting on his fingers as he continued, "A heart attack took my father without warning. My only brother and his family were killed when their wagon overturned in the river. My sister's husband died at Gettysburg, and grief drove her to an early grave. My wife and unborn child were killed by a soldier's stray bullet intended for a deserting soldier, leaving my other children motherless. And for what? Why hadn't the Lord interceded? Why hadn't He done something to save her and our baby?"

Valerie saw the pain, still bright in his dark eyes, that his memories awakened. "I'm so sorry, Paul," she said. "I never meant to open old wounds."

As though she hadn't said a word, Paul closed his eyes and recited another Bible verse. "*God is faithful, who will not suffer you to be tempted above that ye are able; but will with the temptation also make a way to escape, that ye may be able to bear it.*'"

"First Corinthians chapter ten, verse thirteen," she said. "Once upon a time, I *did* have faith. I trusted and believed, and, like you, I prayed myself hoarse. But God didn't answer. What was I to think, except that I wasn't deserving of an answer? He looked into my heart and my mind, heard my thoughts and doubts, even as I prayed, and saw how undeserving I was. *That's* why He didn't answer my prayers, Paul. *That's* why He allowed everyone I loved to be taken from me."

Paul sighed, long and loud. "You couldn't be more wrong. Life has made you strong, but I believe that your strength has hardened your heart to the Lord's true message."

Valerie opened her mouth to argue, but he pressed on. "You say you're not good when, in reality, you have more good in your little finger than most of us have in our entire bodies."

She wrinkled her nose over that one, and he watched her bite back bitter tears, which touched a long-forgotten chord in his heart. Rita had been a woman who cried often and easily. She'd been sheltered from pain and suffering to the extent that every time they touched her, even in a small way, tears somehow soothed her.

Valerie wasn't like that. She'd stiffened her back to tragedy instead of giving in to it. She'd marched headlong into life despite all she'd lost. Somehow, he had to make her see that the strength she took such pride in was God's gift to her—His way of sheltering her from further pain and suffering.

Paul wanted to hold her close. To soothe her with gentle kisses and tender touches. To tell her what a rare and valuable person she was. *All in good time*, he told himself. *All in good time.*

"You think no one knows who's been putting food and clothes and shoes on the children's doorsteps?" Paul said instead. "You think folks don't realize who paid for all those wonderful books that have lined the schoolhouse shelves since you came to town?" He took her hands in his and clasped them tightly. "You think we aren't aware it's been *you* buying slates and chalk and paper and pencils, and telling the children the supplies are being paid for by the school district? You did those good things because you believed they needed to be done.

"What's more, you've made great personal sacrifices to do these things. And you did them in a quiet, Christian way, so that no one felt beholden, so that no one was embarrassed by a lack of money." After a long pause, he added, "The only question is, how does that great big heart of yours fit into that tiny little body?"

"But—but I was so careful to stay out of sight!" Valerie stammered. "I didn't want anyone feeling beholden to me—"

"It's my personal belief that Mr. Daniel Webster studied you before he defined the word *good*," Paul said, smiling when his comment turned her cheeks bright pink. "I can't assume to understand all you've gone through to make you believe as you do, but I can tell you this: the Lord loves you. He knows what you've suffered, and He understands your anger. He *made* you, don't forget...."

She took a deep breath and glanced in the direction of the store. "Greta will think I've lost my mind," she said, giggling nervously. "I paid for my groceries, then walked away without them!"

"You can pretend our little conversation never took place, if you must," he said, "but you can't pretend you didn't hear me. You *are* a good woman, Valerie Carter, and God sees the goodness that originates from your heart. Someday, you'll believe that."

"Thank you for your kind words," she said, one hand on his forearm. "I don't deserve them, but thank you, anyway."

"Don't you own a mirror?"

Her brow furrowed with confusion.

"Can't you see what a remarkable woman you are?" The question made her blush again.

"Paul, please—I—"

He held up a hand to silence her. "Do me a favor, will you?"

She nodded.

"I know you have a Bible in your house, hidden away somewhere. Dust it off and read my favorite verse, Romans 8:35." With that, he stood up, turned on his heel, and headed for his buckboard, which had been loaded with supplies and was waiting near the steps of the feed and grain. He didn't look at her again until he urged the horse forward, and when he did, Paul knew without a doubt that he loved her.

Weeks passed before she saw him again. She missed his easy smile. His sparkling, coffee-colored eyes. The insistent, wayward curl on his forehead that refused to stay tucked beneath his black felt cap. *Why,* Valerie thought, smiling, *I even love that silly cap that he probably wears to bed!*

She'd done what he'd asked of her, albeit not immediately. She knew exactly where she'd stored the Good Book. When she finally lifted the fire-blackened lid of the huge oak trunk, she sank to the floor and wept bitter, lonely tears. These few articles were all that was left of her happy, close-knit family.

Valerie carefully lifted the Bible from its resting place so as not to loosen any of the pages charred by the fire that had leveled Carter Hall. Slumping into her rocker and leaning against the headrest, she held the Bible to her cheek. It still smelled faintly of smoke. The odor, along with the softness of the leather cover against her cheek, took her back in time to the day she'd tried desperately to forget—but couldn't.

She'd just returned from her mother's burial.

Mama would have no marker for her grave for a very long time because the Yankees had destroyed the stonemason's shop. So, Valerie had fashioned a crude, wooden cross the night before the funeral and, using her father's pocketknife, had carved,

> *Here lies Mandy Carter,*
> *beloved wife and mother.*
> *1825–1863*

She hadn't remembered to take a hammer, however, and had been forced to hunt the cemetery grounds for a large rock to use, instead, to pound the cross into the ground. She also hadn't thought to make a point on the end of the cross, and it had ended up taking her nearly an hour to get the marker to stand upright by her mother's grave.

There wouldn't be any of the typical after-service chatter over pie and coffee, for the good folks of her church had much to do, thanks to the Yankees. And it had been just as well, because Valerie had needed to prepare herself. When she'd finished and had begun walking home, she'd realized that it would be the first time in her life that she'd go home to an empty house. The first time in her life she'd be totally alone. She'd refused all offers of a ride home, preferring instead to walk the three miles in quiet solitude.

Valerie hadn't noticed the flaming glow on the horizon until she'd made the final turn that would lead her to the manor house. At first, the orange haze had confused her. She'd read about comets and meteors and such, and she'd wondered, for a moment, if maybe one had fallen to earth. But the closer she'd come to the house, the more aware she'd become that no comet or meteor had caused the day sky to glare in that way.

With tears in her eyes and a sob in her throat, Valerie had run as fast as her booted feet would carry her—down the magnolia-lined drive, across the bridge that crossed a small tributary of the James River, which divided Carter Hall in two, and past the grassy knoll, which led to the wide, welcoming porch....

But the porch was gone.

And so were the heavy, oak double doors.

Yankee soldiers were everywhere, it seemed—some on horseback, others standing, a few sprawled on the lawn like Fourth of July celebrants watching a fireworks display.

Valerie had frozen in her tracks, mesmerized by the flames eating her home and her heritage, board by board and brick by brick. It wasn't till the last ember had died, in the wee hours of the morning, that she'd realized her cheeks had been singed by the powerful heat of the blaze. Soot had grayed the lace trim of her black mourning dress, and flecks of ash had gathered on her shoulders and in her hair.

The soldiers, bored now that the best of the show had ended, had wandered off to see what valuables could be hoisted from the ruins. And Valerie, dazed and confused, had stood shock-silent in the rubble that had once been her mother's lovely, ornately decorated parlor.

When a Yankee soldier had asked her why she was crying over things that represented slavery and oppression, Valerie had marched right up to him and, despite the fact that he'd towered over her like Jack's giant, slapped his face with all the strength she'd been able to muster.

"Slavery was *never* tolerated at Carter Hall!" she'd shouted. "My father gave his *life* defending his workers' freedom!"

She'd shoved the burly man, then had pointed over his shoulder toward the remnants of the tidy white cottages that had flanked the long, winding drive. "See those houses over there? Once, there were twenty of them, and every farm hand had a garden plot behind his house. And a tool shed. They earned fair wages and were free to come and go as they pleased. And see there?" she'd asked, pointing again. "That was our schoolhouse, and all of our field hands and their children learned to read and write there, regardless of the color of their skin!"

"Sorry, miss, that the stench of smoke and charred wood has filled your pretty green eyes with tears…."

She'd never been a violent sort. Why, it had always made her heart ache if Lee Junior or Delbert had so much as squashed a spider beneath his boot heel. But the arrogance of this man, defending an army that had destroyed everything she'd held dear, had made her want to commit violence. Instead, Valerie had summoned the last of her calm. "What city do you call home, soldier?"

Smiling uncomfortably at her angry interrogation, he'd answered, "Boston."

"When you return North to a family that loves you and a home that doesn't have a 'stench of smoke and charred wood,'" she'd hissed, "will you sleep well, knowing what you've done here on Southern soil? Do you truly believe in what you fought for, soldier? Or did you put on that pretty blue uniform just to collect a dependable salary at the end of every month?"

He'd been standing there, blinking like a simpleton, when two of his buddies had called him to join them. Suddenly, as if the shame of war and the hatred that inspires it had enveloped him, the soldier had slung his pack over his shoulder. Tears had misted in his own bloodshot eyes, and he'd said softly, "I know 'sorry' won't do you any good now, but I'm mighty sorry, just the same."

And he'd left her standing there, the last in a long line of proud Carters, alone and surrounded by the shadowy remnants of Carter Hall Plantation.

Valerie had waited until the line of Bluecoats had disappeared into the wooded glen at the north end of the property before tiptoeing through what had been the keeping room, where her father used to tell her stories about when he was a boy, then around what had been the kitchen, where only a few blackened bricks from the wall-wide fireplace had lain in a sloppy heap. She'd wandered into what had been her father's library, where the walls were once lined with green, maroon, brown, and black leather-bound books of all shapes and sizes.

A few books had survived the fire.

Among them had been the family Bible.

It had still been warm and smoldering when she'd picked it up, its cover dulled and dirty, its gold-edged pages singed and curled, and she'd clutched it to her breast and fallen to her knees, sobbing so loud and so hard that she'd wondered if the Yankees would turn about-face to see what wounded animal to put out of its misery.

She'd held the Good Book in both hands, raised it to the heavens, and cried aloud, "Why, Lord? *Why?*"

She had waited, but no answer had come. But then, she'd needed no booming voice to resound from the clouds. She'd known why God hadn't answered.

It was because she hadn't deserved an answer.

She'd lived a life of luxury from the day she was born. Surrounded by riches, Valerie had never wanted for anything, not even for a moment. Perhaps, the Lord thought she'd grown selfish and self-centered, that she should have shared more of her riches with those less fortunate.

The truth was, she'd never even thought of it. Her father had struggled his whole life to protect her from the ugly things in the world, and she'd never seen—let alone experienced—pain and suffering. Mama was her warmth, and Papa was her strength. Lee Junior and Delbert, her protectors.

Then, one by one, they'd been taken from her.

Forever.

If not for her grandmother's entries in the front of the Bible and those few treasures she'd dug from the smoking ruins, Valerie would have nothing but memories of them.

So, yes, she had avoided fulfilling Paul's request to look up the Bible verse, at first, because she'd touched the Good Book before and knew it would only awaken carefully buried feelings of pain and loneliness. Worse, it would awaken carefully buried feelings of anger—anger toward the God who had allowed all her suffering to take place in order to teach a hard lesson to a selfish young woman.

Now, something she remembered about Paul's tone of voice made her open the Bible. Automatically, as if she hadn't avoided the verse these many months, she turned to Romans 8:35 and read aloud in a trembling voice, *"Who shall separate us from the love of Christ?"*

Only you can do that, said a tiny voice deep within her heart. Silently, she read the last two verses in chapter eight: *"I am persuaded, that neither death, nor life, nor angels, nor principalities, nor powers, nor things present, nor things to come, nor height, nor depth, nor any other creature, shall be able to separate us from the love of God, which is in Christ Jesus our Lord."*

Not even my own stubborn, hardened heart? she wondered.

Valerie closed the Bible so softly that it made no sound at all, then leaned back in the rocker and closed her eyes. A sense of being surrounded by love and acceptance rolled over her like a giant, gentle wave. For the first time in years, she knew peace in her heart, and she fell asleep, smiling the sweet, contented smile of a carefree baby.

Chapter Seven

I t was the worst winter on record, with ice, wind, and snow that piled up to the windowsills. Richmond often became cold between November and February, but Valerie couldn't remember ever seeing anything quite like this.

When the first snow fell in early December, she felt like a small child trying hard to act grown up, for every few minutes, she found herself standing at the window overlooking the back yard and grinning foolishly as the faded green grass turned into a white blanket of snow. From the front porch, Valerie continued to watch in awe as the flakes floated from the sky and alighted, whisper-soft, one atop the next, on the ground. And, like a child sneaking cookies before supper, she waited until after dark to step out into it. By then, six inches had accumulated on the ground.

She chased Scruffy through the snow, tossed snowballs at him, and allowed him to kick showers of it at her. Lucky for her, the evidence of their romp was hidden by morning beneath another six inches of snow. The world took on a whole new look, covered in white—it was hushed and velvety, peaceful and pure.

That snowfall caused the school to close for the first time that winter—and additional snowfalls caused it to close seven more times that same month. The awesome beauty of the snow had diminished along about the fourth snowfall, even in Valerie's snow-awed eyes. By Christmas, Freeland was white for as far as the eye could see. Valerie had never had a white Christmas, and she looked forward to waking up to a snowy landscape on that great morning.

Freelanders, she discovered, made a big fuss over the day. For weeks beforehand, prayer groups, choir rehearsals, and decorating and baking parties abounded. Gifts of homemade jellies and preserves, delicious breads and cakes, hand-carved wooden decoys, and more were exchanged among friends and neighbors. The presents went back and forth so quickly that Valerie jokingly said it was the gift exchange, and not Mother Nature, that caused the high winds whipping up and down Main Street.

Church services the Sunday before Christmas were reverent yet festive. Hymns and carols sung by the children's choir warmed the little church building almost as surely as the crackling fire in the huge potbelly stove, and Rev. Gemmill's sermon made the parishioners feel as if they were there in Bethlehem beneath the great star, awaiting the birth of their Savior.

Valerie happily joined in the rituals and customs of Christmas in Freeland, for she was more than the town schoolmarm—now, she was a real member of the community. Freeland had become much more than just the place where she lived. It was home, and the people who lived there were her family.

The anger she'd harbored in her heart after losing her parents, her brothers, and her home had lessened, day by day, gradually being replaced by the warm acceptance of God's love. Paul had been right when he'd told her she didn't have to earn that love, but Valerie felt a strong sense of duty toward the Lord, anyway. And with that duty, she felt an obligation to spend the rest of her days earning the Creator's forgiveness; just as she believed He understood that grief and loneliness had caused her spiteful anger, she believed He deserved nothing but her best.

So, now, when she attended a church service, Valerie listened intently to Rev. Gemmill's sermon. She started and ended every day by reading God's Word. And between the hours of sunrise and sunset, Valerie found herself conversing more easily with Him.

Prayer came naturally now that she'd found her way back to Him.

And she'd found her way back thanks to Paul Collins.

No one could have given her a greater gift, and she loved Paul all the more for it.

So, on Christmas Day, when Rev. and Mrs. Gemmill opened the church, where turkeys and hams, vats of stuffing and yams, and huge bowls of mashed potatoes and gravy lined the long, narrow tables in the church cellar, she sought out his handsome face. That wasn't an easy task, since every Freelander, it seemed, showed up at precisely the same time for the biggest Christmas party Valerie had ever attended.

Early in the day, she was chatting with Greta when Paul and the children whisked her away to the far corner of the meeting room, where they insisted that she shut her eyes tightly and let them lead her into the church's foyer. When at last they told her to open her eyes, she found herself looking at the prettiest rocking chair she'd ever seen.

"I carved the spindles," Tyler crowed, pointing at the rods connecting the sturdy legs to one another, "and Pa caned the chair's seat and back."

"It was me put the little iron brads on the feet," Timmy chimed in. "Used Pa's hammer an' did 'em all by myself! An' Tricia made the cushion so it would match the curtains in your parlor."

Valerie ran her fingertips along the smooth arms of the oak rocker. "I don't think I've ever seen a lovelier piece of furniture," she said, settling into it. "And I know I've never sat in a more comfortable chair."

Paul's grin, which broadened with her compliments, lit up the room. "The young'uns told me they once saw you hammerin' the rockers back onto the chair you have now," he said, twisting his cap in his hands. "It was their idea to make you a new one...."

And what a perfect gift it was. Valerie knew that it had taken many hours to cut and carve and polish the honey-gold wood. The fact that they'd gone to such trouble and given so much time for her brought tears to her eyes.

"Golly, Pa," Timmy said, wrinkling his nose, "I thought you said she'd like it." He gave the matter a moment's thought, then added, "And didn't *she* just say that she liked it?"

Valerie wiped her eyes and tried to compose herself.

"Don't you know nothin' 'bout women?" Tyler whispered to his little brother. "She likes it just fine. It's just that women sometimes cry when they're happy. Ain't that so, Pa?"

"*Isn't* that so?" Tricia corrected him. "Right, Miss Carter?"

Valerie sniffed and nodded. "That's absolutely correct, Tricia." She focused on Timmy and said, "Tyler is right, too, when he says that sometimes women cry when they're happy. And I want you to know that I'm happy now. Very, very happy."

Timmy's blue eyes widened. "Well, don't that just beat all."

"It does seem ridiculous, doesn't it?" Valerie agreed.

Paul laughed and mussed Timmy's hair. "Go on over there and get in the food line," he said to his children. "Save Miss Carter and your old pa a place, won't you?"

Once the children were out of earshot, Paul squatted down beside Valerie and took her hands in his. "I hoped you'd like it."

Being eye to eye with him, Valerie could not mistake the glow of love that emanated from his face. "It'll bring me hours of comfort," she said. "It's such a thoughtful and generous gift. I don't deserve—"

Paul held up a hand. "Why are you always forcing me to shush you with those silly notions of yours?" he asked. "You *do* deserve it! Why, you've been...." He paused, searching, it seemed, for the right words. "You taught my young'uns to smile and be happy again. What a wonderful addition you've been to their lives!"

Valerie waited breathlessly, hoping he'd add, "You've been a wonderful addition to *my* life, too." When several seconds ticked by without a word between them, she said, "Speaking of the children, I suppose we ought to join them...."

His eyes never left hers as he nodded his agreement. "I suppose," he said, still holding her hand as she stood up. He released it only when they began to cross the room.

They walked, side by side, to where his three children were standing in a gaggle of other youngsters waiting to get their share of the Christmas meal. "We thought you were gonna sit there all day," Timmy said, his tiny finger teasingly poking his father in the tummy. "Tyler says you're 'moon-eyed' over Miss Carter. What's it mean, Pa?"

Paul's face flushed. He looked from Valerie to his son and back again, twisting his hat in his hands the whole time.

"It means," Valerie said, deliberately and calmly, "that he likes me." She winked at Paul. "Which is very good news to me, because I like him, too."

Greta, who'd been standing in line ahead of them, turned suddenly. "Da two of you ain't foolin' nobody," she said, clucking her tongue. Then, elbowing Paul's ribs, she winked. "Mebbe ve vill haff a June vedding, yah?"

Paul's blush deepened, and Valerie looked away to hide her own flushed face. But not for long. She felt obliged to rescue him from Greta's well-intentioned yet intrusive joke. "Oh, Greta," Valerie teased, "there can't be a June wedding, because Mr. Collins and I have taken permanent vows of chastity."

Greta chuckled. "Yah. Sure. Und dere's a man in der moon who eats green cheese all da day long, too!" With that, she stepped up to the food table and began filling her plate.

"You're going to sit with us, aren't you?" Timmy asked Valerie.

She glanced at Paul and saw the same question in his dark eyes. "Why, I'd love to join you for dinner," she said, smiling.

No one said another word about Greta's comments as they ate. It felt good, Valerie thought, sitting across from Paul at one of the smaller tables and listening to the sweet chatter of his children. It felt familiar and warm. It felt *right*.

The day went on merrily, with moments of prayer and time for games, as well as a special nativity performance put on by the children. But all too soon, the farewells began to float around the homey basement space of the church. Valerie had made sure to spend some time with all of her students and their families. She'd done her share of serving food and cleaning up. She'd played games and sung songs and prayed. Surrounded by all this warmth, she hated the prospect of returning alone to her little house. She wished the day never had to end.

As she shrugged resignedly into her cloak, Paul stepped up behind her and smoothed the dark, woolen garment over her shoulders. "I thought I'd walk home with you," he said, quickly adding, "so I can carry the chair for you, of course."

Valerie smiled, glad he'd sought her out. Glad he wanted to spend these last few minutes of this very special day alone with her. "How thoughtful, Paul. That would be lovely," she admitted.

They trudged along the snow-covered street, chatting about the delicious foods and playful games that were part and parcel of a Freeland Christmas as they went. Now and then, Paul put the chair down to renew his grip on it. Once, when he did, Valerie sat down, telling him she needed a short nap after all the pie she'd eaten. Much to her surprise, he lifted her, chair and all, and resumed walking and talking as though she were still moving alongside him. Only when she threatened to jump over the side of the chair did he stop and let her down.

Inside her home, Paul held the chair as Valerie lit a lantern in the parlor. "Where would you like me to put it?" he asked.

Valerie bit her lower lip and scanned the room, then shoved her old rocker aside. "I can read and sew and grade papers in it," she said, "right here by the warmth and light of the fire."

He slid the new chair into place. "Guess I ought to get back to the church and round up those young'uns. They'll probably be sound asleep before I get 'em home."

Valerie recalled how Paul's children had fallen asleep in the back of his wagon after the church picnic the previous summer. "It's been quite a day," she said. "I'm sure they're exhausted."

Paul took a few hesitant steps toward the door, then turned to face her. He opened his mouth to speak, but no sound came out. With one hand on the doorknob, he took a deep breath. "What Greta said," he began, "...I hope it didn't embarrass you too badly."

Valerie licked her lips. *Embarrass me?* she thought. Why, the woman couldn't have paid her a greater compliment than to suggest Valerie was wife material for a man like Paul! "Of course, I wasn't embarrassed," she admitted quietly. "In fact, I was quite flattered."

Paul sighed, then smiled. "Good," he said. "Because, I must admit, the idea is appealing...."

Blinking, Valerie took a gulp of air as he crossed the room in two long strides and wrapped her in his arms. "Merry Christmas, Valerie Carter," he whispered into her hair. "A very merry Christmas."

She looked up into his handsome face. "And the same to you, Paul Collins."

When he kissed her, she thought she knew what it would feel like to float on a summer breeze. To ride a wave on a stormy sea. Yet there, in the protective circle of his strong arms, she felt safe and secure.

She felt *loved.*

"There are worse things," he said, holding her at arm's length, "wouldn't you say?"

Still reeling from the surprise of his kiss, Valerie took a deep breath. "Worse than what?"

"Worse than being with a man like me, a time-worn, work-hardened father of three."

He read the long silence that followed as a polite rejection and loosened his hold on her. *Too much, too soon,* he told himself, taking half a step back. Just because *he'd* thought and prayed endlessly about this moment didn't mean that Valerie was ready to respond affirmatively right away to his half-baked proposal.

He looked into her pretty face. Into her bright, long-lashed eyes, which glowed like emeralds in the soft lamplight. At the tendrils of shining hair that refused to stay pinned in the bun she'd twisted atop her head. This time, when he kissed her, he wanted the kiss to say what he didn't have the courage to speak aloud: *If the day ever comes when you love me even half as much as I love you, it'll be the answer to a prayer.*

"I have a little something for you, too," Valerie said after their kiss, breaking away and ducking into her room. "I didn't bring it to the church because I had two brothers, and I remember how awkward men can feel when they're the center of attention."

They stood on either side of her new rocker, Valerie grinning nervously as his big hands tore away the red bow and white paper from his present. For a moment, he only stared at it. "No one ever knitted me a jacket before."

"I thought it would help keep you warm as you tend the animals on cold winter mornings...."

Smiling, Paul shook his head. "You're amazing."

Blushing, Valerie said, "I hope it fits."

He held the thick, gray-green knit against his chest. "It's perfect. But it must have taken months to make, what with all your other duties...."

She shrugged. "An hour or two, here and there." She paused. "But if it had taken months, it'd have been worth every moment."

Paul draped the jacket across one arm of the rocker and stepped around the chair to take her in his arms. "It's one of the most thoughtful gifts I've ever received, and it'll keep me warm even when I'm not wearing it."

The month of January brought frigid temperatures and four more blizzards. By February, every road and walkway looked like a tunnel that had been carved between six-foot snowdrifts. The skies seemed endlessly white, with snow clouds looming overhead and threatening to dump even more of the dread white stuff on the tiny town. By March, the few folks who were able to brave the slick streets complained to Greta in the feed and grain about the horrible weather conditions. Even Mr. Talbot groaned that in all his years, he hadn't seen such a winter. "An' I'm nigh-on to a hunnert years old!"

"Ole Mudder Nature must be mad as a hornet vit us to be punishing us so diss year," joked the shopkeeper.

But Valerie found nothing funny about the harsh weather. She hadn't seen her students in weeks.

Worse, she hadn't seen Paul in weeks. She missed him more than she'd imagined it possible to miss anyone.

One morning, as the first light of day peeped over the window-sill, Scruffy's barking caught her attention. Valerie got out of bed, dressed quickly, and headed outside.

"What's all the racket about?" she asked the dog.

Scruffy only continued to whimper and paw at the ground.

Once she reached his side, Valerie understood. "Why, you silly thing, you. You'd think you'd never seen a crocus before!" she said, patting his head. "Isn't it wonderful! It's a sure sign that spring is right around the corner."

Hunkering down, she leaned nearer the cluster of purple- and yellow-striped blossoms. Their faint fragrance wafted into her nostrils, and she stayed there on her hands and knees in the cold snow for what seemed like an hour before she'd had enough of it.

"Lose somethin'?"

The rich, masculine voice startled Valerie such that she lost her balance and ended up facedown in the flower bed. "Josh Kent," she scolded, ignoring his hearty laughter, "you scared the daylights out of me. What're you doing here at this hour?"

"I heard that mutt of yours all the way down to the jailhouse," the town sheriff answered. "Thought maybe something had happened to you from the way he was carryin' on."

Valerie stood up and brushed the snow from her hands and knees. "I suppose I ought to thank you for your concern," she said, smiling, "but I'm grateful you decided to become a sheriff instead of a doctor. What a bedside manner you'd have!"

Josh's laughter floated around her snow-covered yard. ` on't suppose you'd have a cup of coffee for a sleepy old bachelor, would you?"

"No, but I could whip one up, if you don't mind keeping me company while I do."

Josh followed her up the walk and into the house. "Don't mind a bit. It's not every day a fella has an opportunity to chat with a pretty young lady."

And chat they did. About the dreadful winter. About the spring thaw. About preparations for the upcoming Easter celebration at the church. She'd been in Freeland six months, and Josh had been one of the first citizens to welcome her to town. He made a point of visiting her regularly, just to see if she needed lamp oil or firewood. She was surprised to learn, there at her kitchen table, that Josh played the part of Jesus in the Passion play every year.

"Well, I figure they picked me that first year because of my beard," he said, stroking the hairy growth on his chin.

But Valerie knew better; she'd heard him sing. "It's that baritone that sold them on you. I'll bet you could sing opera if you had a mind to."

Under his thick, dark beard, Josh blushed. "I do enjoy making music with this here instrument God gave me." He told her there was no one to sing Mary Magdalene's part in this year's production. "Missy Putnam used to do it, but she moved on up to Shrewsbury when she married that Marcus boy." He swallowed the last of his coffee, then leaned closer to Valerie. "Don't suppose you'd be interested in the part, would you?"

Valerie giggled and held a hand to her chest. "Me? Why, I couldn't carry a tune in a basket."

Josh shook his head. "Now, don't you be modest with me, Valerie Carter. I've stood in the pew in front of you at church, an'

I don't recollect ever hearin' anybody sing 'Rock of Ages' quite as pretty as you."

Valerie tucked in one corner of her mouth. "That's different, Josh. It's easy to sing when your voice is just one in a crowd. But when it's the only one...."

"Why not give it a try?" he prompted her. "Bein' in the play is a real hoot, I'll tell you. An' the reverend's wife cooks a special dinner for anyone who's part of the Passion play...."

Valerie had sung several solos at Harvester Baptist in Richmond, but she had been younger then. Younger and braver and....

"So, whaddya say, Valerie? Will you do it?"

Sighing, she rolled her eyes.

"We'll have to cancel the whole thing if we can't find somebody to do those songs," he persisted. "They're central to the story, y'know...."

"What about Emma Thompson? She has a lovely voice."

Josh shook his head. "Nope. She just gave birth to twin boys, remember? Why, I doubt she'll have time to *attend* the play, let alone be part of it."

"Sue Rosen?"

"Now, I don't like soundin' mean-spirited, Valerie, but why on earth would you want to do that to all those innocent folks? Sue sounds more like a squeaky hinge than a gal when she sings."

"There must be someone—"

"Looky here. The real reason I stopped by, Valerie, wasn't to see what your old dog was a-barkin' about. It was to ask if you'd agree to do this favor for us. I'm on a mission, y'might say. See...I'm the official choir spokesman."

She raised her brows and blinked in shock. "You mean...."

"Yup. The reverend himself asked for you. Now, how can you turn down an invitation like that?"

Paul had never heard anything more beautiful in his life. He'd been told that, in years past, Missy Putnam had always done well with the melodies for the Passion play, but, listening to Valerie's rendition of the songs, Paul thought he knew what the poets meant when they wrote about angels' voices. The sound issued from her as smoothly as wind slipped through the willows. She sang with her eyes closed, her hands clasped in front of her, and her soft, melodic tones caught everyone's full attention. Even the babies stopped crying, as if the sound of Valerie's voice was soothing them into sleepy silence.

For a moment, as Valerie stood there in front of her fellow parishioners, wearing the blue gown and veil fashioned for her by Jan Bugg, Paul got a picture of her snuggled in the oak rocker he'd made for her, cradling an infant in her arms as she hummed sweet lullabies into its innocent face.

He blinked himself out of the daydream and chastised himself severely. She'd been through a lot in her short life. If he wanted her as his own, he'd have to be patient. He'd have to take his time.

Paul smiled. He wasn't a rich man. He didn't live in a mansion or own a plantation, and, very likely, he never would. He didn't have much money in the bank. But he had time.

Time was the one thing he had a whole lot of.

When the Passion play ended, it took a full fifteen minutes for Paul to elbow his way up to the front of the church to see Valerie. Even then, the two of them were surrounded by the rest of the choir. He sent a silent prayer heavenward. *Lord, if it's Your will, I'll ask her to marry me. Just show me the way so I'll do it according to Your plan for her life and mine.... But first, You have to do me a favor and clear the way, please.*

It didn't surprise him in the least when he and Valerie suddenly found themselves alone at the front of the church. "You were wonderful," Paul said, his fingertips grazing her cheek.

"I was scared out of my wits."

He laughed. "That was *fear* I heard? Why, I thought the tremolo was part of your natural voice."

She laughed, too. "Don't I wish!" Then, "Do you really think I did all right? You don't think I was too loud? Or too quiet? Could you understand all of the words? The lyrics are so lovely, so meaningful, don't you agree? I'd hate to think I'd rushed through them, because folks should get the full impact of what the writer was trying to express," she rambled nervously.

"Well, haven't *you* come a long way in a short time?"

Valerie drew her brows together as she removed the blue veil from her head and draped it over her arm. "I beg your pardon?"

"Just a few months ago, you were positive the Lord hadn't answered any of your prayers because He didn't love you; today, you're concerned that perhaps one of His children missed the true message of the songs. Do I take that to mean you now believe yourself worthy of His love?"

For a moment, she only stared at him. Then, a slow, easy smile spread across her face. "Yes," she whispered. "I believe it now. It's a wonderful feeling, and I have you to thank for helping me find my way back."

Paul shook his head. "You'd have found your way on your own, eventually, I'm sure."

"Well, that's neither here nor there, now, is it?" she asked, winking. "The fact of the matter is, your persistence softened my cold little heart."

He slipped an arm around her waist and led her down the center aisle of the church toward the double doors, thinking of a day in the future when they'd be taking the same walk. He grinned. "Let me remind you that your heart may be a lot of things, Valerie Carter, but cold is surely not one of them."

Chapter Eight

N ow, class," Valerie said, "turn to page forty-eight in your geography books, please." She waited patiently, listening to the quiet shuffling of feet as the children reached under their chairs for their books before flipping through the pages to find the one she'd indicated.

She couldn't help but smile, for she loved each and every one of them almost as much as she would had she given birth to them herself. It felt so good to have them all back at the same time that she found it easy to put the miserable winter out of her mind.

If only Abel Johnson's murder were as easy to forget, she thought, distracted for a moment by Abel Junior, who was sitting up front and grinning for her approval.

Valerie couldn't put her finger on it, but she felt an ominous presence in town. She'd felt it very strongly ever since Abel was hanged by the Klan. For a reason she couldn't explain, she believed the Klan members responsible for his death had moved into Freeland quietly, the way rattlers slither under rocks, ready to strike, unbeknownst to those who tread by. The feeling had diminished some during the harsh winter, but she suspected that was because the Klansmen didn't like nasty weather any more than the good folks of Freeland did.

All through the day, as she taught her students about the geography of Europe, as she showed them how to multiply and divide, as she read to them from *Great Expectations,* her fear grew inside her. And though she prayed it away every time, it came right back, like the bad penny her grandmother had always teased her about.

Valerie suspected that whatever was causing her turmoil couldn't be shed as easily as a bad penny.

Less than a week later, her worst fears were realized.

Ardith Johnson, who'd been working as a cook at the Freelander Hotel since Abel's death, had finally saved up enough money to move into a small house at the end of Main Street. After the family had been forced from their home, Rev. Gemmill had allowed Ardith to store her furniture in the church basement, and when the day came to take up residence in her new home, half the men in the parish showed up to help her move in, while their wives provided cool, refreshing drinks and filling sandwiches. By the end of the day, the congregants of St. John the Baptist church were only too happy to let the reverend lead them in a "Praise the Lord this day is over!" prayer.

Valerie could see Ardith's new house from her front porch, and as she turned out her lamp for the night, she couldn't help but grin with satisfaction as she looked across at the warm glow in the windows. It was only fair and right that Ardith and her children had a chance to turn things around for themselves. It was God's answer to the prayers of Ardith's friends that had given them that chance. Her final thought after a day of worry was the satisfaction of answered prayer.

In the middle of the night, her deep, peaceful slumber was disturbed by a shrill scream. Valerie pulled on her robe and rushed to the window to look outside into the darkness.

There, in the middle of Main Street, was a row of men on horseback. Their white hoods and robes matched the coverings on their horses, and the torches they held cast an eerie glow over the town.

"Put up the cross!" shouted the man out front. A large, oddly shaped medallion hung from a thick chain around his neck, marking him, Valerie supposed, as the leader of this pack of savage men. Two of the others jumped down from their horses, while a third man held the reins. In the blink of an eye, a huge, wooden cross had been jammed into the ground in front of Ardith's house.

"Get the coal oil!" the leader hollered. "Soak it! Soak it good!"

Again, his band of evil men followed his orders.

"And now," the leader said, "let the light of Christ burn bright. Let them see and understand that it is not God's plan for niggers to be equal to white men or to live among us." He touched his torch to the foot of the cross and leaped back as flames shot skyward.

Valerie had never seen a more horrifying sight. That anyone could connect the crucifix upon which the Lord Jesus had given His life for all mankind with something as vile and wretched as this turned her stomach.

"Bring the nigger woman here before me!" the leader ordered. "She will be taught a lesson about God's hierarchy on this night!"

Are they going to kill Ardith as they killed Abel? Valerie wondered frantically. *Will her children be forced to watch their mother suffer at the hands of these barbarians, just as they watched their father murdered?*

Valerie could not stand by and allow such a thing to happen. Hurriedly, she stepped into a skirt and boots and, without even bothering to close the door behind her, dashed into the street.

"Stop it!" she cried, running toward the men. "Stop right now!"

The leader crossed both arms over his broad chest. "Go back into your house, Miss Carter," he said. "This is no place for a young lady."

"I will *not* go inside!" she shouted. "I won't let you touch a hair on Ardith's head!"

His laughter grated in her ears like sandpaper. "Little lady," he said, "there's not a blessed thing you can do to stop us."

Two of the Klansmen half carried, half dragged a kicking, screaming Ardith from her new home. Her children ran behind him, crying and reaching out for their mother.

Valerie ran to them and hugged each one. "Go back inside," she said in as soothing a voice as she could muster under the circumstances. "I won't let them hurt her."

Abel Junior, tall for his twelve years, said to his siblings, "Get on inside, now, or I'll tan your hides. I mean it. Scat, now!"

His little brother and sister inched backward, their fingers in their mouths and their dark eyes wide with fright. "Go on!" Abel Junior repeated. "And lock that door behind you when you get inside!"

"You should go with them, Abel," Valerie said.

"I ain't leavin' my ma. If they plan to do her harm, they'll have to do it over my dead body."

She saw that the boy meant business. "Well, stay beside me, then, and do as I say, you hear?"

Abel nodded.

Together, they scrambled for the burning cross. The Klansmen had already bound and gagged Ardith to a tree nearby, and tears were streaming down her smooth, mahogany-colored cheeks.

Valerie ran forward to comfort her, but brawny arms stopped her. "That's about far enough, Miss Carter," said the leader. "We're about God's business, here. This ain't no place for a woman."

"This isn't God's business," she shrieked. "It's the devil's work you're doing!"

Again, his nasty laugh grated in her ears. "You see why females must never be allowed a voice in the church or the government?" he asked his followers. "They don't know what's good for 'em—even the ones what teach our children!" Then, to Valerie, he said, "All right, Miss Carter, it seems you aim to witness what we must do. But you'll do it from the sidelines." He handed her off to the nearest Klansman. "Hold her tight, now," he instructed. "I don't want her interrupting my work."

"Let go of her, you big oaf!" Abel shouted. "Let go, or I'll kick you to the end of the street!"

"Why, you little nigger brat!" the Klansman growled. "I'll carve you up like a Thanksgiving turkey if you try." He shoved Abel hard, and the boy ended up in the arms of another Klansman.

"Hold him, too," the leader said. "Maybe it's good that he sees what we're about to do here. It'll teach him what's in store for him if he steps out of line...."

Side by side, Valerie and Abel, held tightly by the white-robed madmen, watched in silent horror as the leader took a long, thick whip from his saddle horn.

Lord, Valerie prayed silently, *guide my tongue. Tell me what to say to stop this madness!* And in the same moment, a Bible verse came to mind: "'O God,'" Valerie shouted, "*the proud are risen against me, and the assemblies of violent men have sought after my soul....*'"

The leader slapped the ground with his whip. "Quoting psalms will not help her. This much I assure you, Miss Carter."

"'*...And have not set thee before them,*'" she continued in an even louder voice. "'*But thou, O* LORD, *art a God full of compassion, and gracious, longsuffering, and plenteous in mercy and truth. O turn unto me, and have mercy upon me; give thy strength unto thy servant....Show me a token for good; that they which hate me may see it, and be ashamed.*'"

It was as if Valerie had not spoken at all. The crack of the whip rang out as the vile thing cut through the cotton of Ardith's white nightgown. The woman did not cry out in pain, as the Klansmen were surely hoping she would. Instead, she stood tall, threw back her shoulders, and quoted a Scripture verse of her own: *"I will love thee, O Lord, my strength. The Lord is my rock, and my fortress, and my deliverer; my God, my strength, in whom I will trust; my buckler, and the horn of my salvation, and my high tower."*

"Shut up!" the leader bellowed. "Shut your yap, nigger woman, or I'll tear every inch of the flesh from your bones, I swear it!"

Ardith's eyes blazed into his as she said, *"'I will call upon the Lord, who is worthy to be praised: so shall I be saved from mine enemies.'"*

"You think so, do you?" the leader yelled. "We'll just see about that!" Again, the wicked slap of the whip tore at Ardith's skin. And again, she did not cry out.

Abel struggled against the grip of the man who was restraining him. "Let my mama go!" he cried. "She ain't done nothin' to you. Why you doin' this? Why?"

The leader stomped over to the boy and glared down into his face. "Why, you ask? I'll tell you why." He pointed past the glowing orange cross to his fellow Klansmen. "We have been called to put the ungodly in their place, that's why. And *you*, boy, are unclean and ungodly."

Just as the leader reached out to grab Abel's throat, a loud voice stopped him. "Don't make me pull this trigger," it said.

The eyes behind the white hood met the angry face of the sheriff, who gave another order. "Untie that woman. Untie her now."

Except for the men holding Valerie and Abel, the Klansmen formed a circle around Josh, their rifles and shotguns aimed at his heart, at his head, at his chest. "You wouldn't shoot me, Josh Kent," the leader said, his voice full of arrogance.

"I will if I have to. Oh, I imagine your puppets here will get off a couple good shots, and I'll likely bite the dust in the process." The sheriff's lopsided grin froze on his face. "But the first bullet outta my little six-shooter here is aimed at your left eyeball. Seems a shame for the both of us to die on such a pretty night, now, don't it?"

No one moved.

No one spoke.

No one dared.

"Uncock your weapons, gentlemen." Josh directed his next comment to the Klan leader in a calm, quiet voice. "If I have to ask you again, I'm afraid there's gonna be a nasty ole bloodstain on that nice, white sheet of yours...."

The faceoff lasted only long enough for the leader to see that Josh was serious. "You'd really die to save this nigger woman?"

"I would," Josh said without hesitation. "Now, untie her."

The leader never took his eyes off Josh. "Do it," he instructed his followers.

"And turn them others loose, too," Josh added.

The men holding Valerie and Abel looked for guidance. When the leader nodded, they pushed their hostages to freedom.

"Don't think this is the end of things," the leader said, mounting his horse. "We have a mission, and we aim to see it through to the end."

As the pack of men rode away, Valerie ran to Ardith and untied her wrists. "Are you all right?" she asked, hugging the woman.

Ardith nodded. "I thought I was a goner for sure," she said, her voice trembling. "If you hadn't come out when you did.... You saved my life, girl."

Valerie ignored the comment. "Abel," she said, "take your mother inside and get her a cool drink of water. I'll be in soon to clean her wounds. Go on, now."

Without a word, Abel led his limping mother back the house. He returned to the doorway for a moment to smile weakly and wave to Valerie. "God bless you, Miss Carter. You saved my mama." With that, he closed and locked the door.

Valerie ignored Abel's comment, too. "Josh," she said, "thank the good Lord you got here when you did. It was *you* who saved Ardith and Abel's lives. You're a hero!"

"Let's have none o' that. I was standin' there long enough to hear you puttin' it to 'em."

"But it was your authority that made them—"

"If you hadn't stalled 'em, I couldn't have done what I did. She'd've been dead long before I got here if you hadn't come out and raised such a ruckus."

Valerie took a deep breath. Only then did she realize she'd been trembling. "I'm going to see about Ardith's injuries. I'm sure she has some tea in the cupboard. Will you join us, Josh?"

She noted a slight tremor in the brave sheriff's hand as he ran it through his thick, dark hair.

Grinning from ear to ear, he holstered his gun and fell into step beside her. "Why, I'd be right proud to share a cup of tea with the bravest woman I've ever met."

All was quiet in town during the following week. The Freelanders, thanks to Josh, had heard what Valerie had done in the dark that night, and, one by one, they'd made it a point to congratulate and thank her.

All but Paul.

What she'd done had been brave, indeed. But it could have cost her her life. For days after he heard the news, he berated himself. If he'd asked her to marry him at Christmas, like he'd planned, she'd have been safe in his house when the incident occurred. On the other hand, he had to admit that if she had been his wife on that terrible night, Ardith Johnson might not have lived to see another day. He wavered between admiring Valerie's bravery and being angry that she'd put her life on the line. Because, bluntly, when she'd stood up for Ardith out there, all alone in the street, she could have been killed. Her death wouldn't have been an accident, as Rita's had, but it wouldn't have been any easier to bear.

He avoided her for two weeks, not knowing how to face her. He was more proud of what she'd done in defending Ardith than he'd ever been of anyone. If only that good feeling would squelch the residual fear of losing her.

Why can't she be more like other women? he wanted to know. *Why can't she be satisfied with a simple life of darning socks and baking pies? Why does she have to be so all-fired involved in life?*

But even as he asked these questions, Paul knew that if Valerie was more like other women, he never would have fallen so completely cap over boots in love with her.

Her independent spirit meant she'd be a true partner, and he knew that, too. She'd never whimper and whine when life tossed its worst at them. She wouldn't stand aside and let him bear the burdens of getting by, day by day, by himself. No, Valerie would shoulder her share. She'd insist on doing so, in fact. She wouldn't notice if Suzie Jackson wore a hand-me-down hat to church. Her conversations wouldn't center on recipe collections and quilt patterns. She wouldn't need to boast about the good deeds she'd done for the church, because the good deeds would be out there in the plain light of day for everyone to see.

Yes, Valerie would be a true partner. And Paul yearned for that—someone who would not only have a hot meal waiting for him when he returned from working the fields all day, but would also have an opinion waiting for him, too. Some of her strength of character would rub off on his children, he knew, and it made him smile just thinking about it.

Most of what he wanted from life, he wanted for his children: A roof over their heads. Three square meals a day. Clean clothes on their backs. But what he wanted for himself was simpler still: a life with Valerie. He'd learn to live with the outbursts of indignation at injustice that prompted her to do things like she'd done for Ardith. Maybe, just maybe, it was part of God's plan for him to teach her a little of what he'd learned about patience.

The very idea made him chuckle. Valerie had come to town freely admitting she'd fallen by the wayside in matters of faith, but when she'd finally found the righteous path again, she'd begun walking straight down the middle of it. No twists and turns in Valerie's road to the Lord! More likely than not, God's plan wasn't for him to teach her about patience at all. More likely than not, God intended to teach *him* a few things—through Valerie.

Paul remembered wishing on the day he'd met her that he could be a boy in school again. If it was true that God would use her to teach him a few things, Paul sensed that the lessons would be learned and never forgotten, and he believed learning would never be more interesting…or fun.

The planting season, like the harvest, very nearly emptied the classroom, much to Valerie's dismay. But living in a farm community required a teacher to be inventive. To be original. To find unique and special ways to ensure that her students wouldn't miss a single lesson.

And so, just as she'd done during the harvest, Valerie started making weekly trips to the absent students' homes, as well as accepting supper invitations to the same tables that had welcomed her before.

She'd nearly finished her meal of fried chicken, mashed potatoes, and snap beans at Andy Cooper's house when she noticed his dad glaring at her from across the table. She blamed his hard days in the fields for his angry, hateful expression. She blamed her many sleepless nights of devising special lesson plans for her heightened sensitivity. She blamed the uncharacteristically hot weather, the lack of rain....

Stodgy and standoffish, Henry Cooper had never been an outgoing man, and Valerie considered herself lucky if she got a polite hello out of him after Sunday services. On previous visits to the Cooper farm, she'd found his wife warm and friendly...but only as long as her husband wasn't around.

Valerie could blame the stars and the moon and the sun, if she wanted to, for Henry's nasty disposition. But she knew in her heart why his beady, brown eyes bored into her as they did, and she knew exactly when it had started.

The previous week, in the leather goods aisle at Greta's, she'd been trying to decide between a pair of brown or black work gloves when Ardith had come into the store. The three women had chatted a while and paid no attention to Henry, picking through the bin of shirts in search of one large enough to hide his huge belly.

It was when he'd turned to give her a full view of his face that Valerie had looked into his eyes and recognized him as the leader of the white-robed gang. The man under the sheet who'd shouted orders like a drill sergeant had had a huge belly, too. Suddenly, Henry had hollered at Greta, "You don't have much of a selection for anybody who's not a beanpole. Next time you put in an order, consider that, why don't you?"

Listening to that voice was like trying to digest ground glass, because it was the very same voice that had ordered Ardith's beating, the voice that likely would have ordered the widow's murder, had Josh Kent not shown up when he did.

Valerie and Ardith had exchanged quick glances. It was obviously by the fear widening the older woman's eyes that she, too, had recognized Henry as one of her captors.

"'The LORD is known by the judgment which he executeth,'" Ardith had whispered, quoting Psalm 9:16; "'the wicked is snared in the work of his own hands.'"

Valerie had grinned at the appropriateness of it. "And by the words from their own mouths," she'd whispered back.

Henry had glowered in their direction. "Women," he'd huffed angrily, "got nothin' important to say. At least you're thoughtful enough not to waste your breath sayin' it loud and wastin' others' time."

"'Be not far from me; for trouble is near,'" Ardith had said.

"You'd better stop that," Valerie had warned her, "or he's liable to—"

"Liable to *what?*" Henry had demanded.

They'd been so busy giggling and whispering that they hadn't heard his approach. Valerie had stood straight and cleared her throat. "Why, Mr. Cooper," she'd said, "I was just telling Ardith what a lovely time I had out at your place last fall. You're very blessed to have such a devoted family."

Frowning, he'd shaken his head and stomped out of the store.

"Have a nice day, Mr. Cooper," Valerie had called after him.

She'd barely heard his grunt of displeasure.

She'd certainly had no idea what it had meant.

At least, not until now, as she sat across from him at his own supper table.

Valerie knew it like she knew her own name. When or where or how, she didn't know, but Henry Cooper meant to make her pay for interfering with his murderous mission.

Chapter Nine

Two uneventful weeks passed, yet Valerie knew better than to let down her guard. She prayed hard and often that if and when Henry struck, she wouldn't be near any of her students.

Every time Andy Cooper was absent from school, she worried his father would take that opportunity to seek vengeance.

But she couldn't let such concerns distract her from her duties. Two of her students, David Garvey and Laura Harper, would graduate this term, and she had a lot to do to get them ready for the big day. The two students agreed to stay after school a couple of days a week to catch up on the work they'd missed during the planting season.

When David had indicated his desire to continue his education, Valerie had contacted some friends in Virginia and secured him a scholarship at the University of Richmond. When he finished college, he'd return to Freeland as a veterinarian. He worked hard to complete his extra assignments.

Laura, on the other hand, was happy just to be finishing school. She was getting married in less than a month, and most of her attentions were focused on final wedding plans.

The three of them were gathered around Valerie's desk one afternoon when what sounded like a herd of stampeding cattle interrupted their studies. Valerie peered out the window to see what had caused all the noise and gasped to see the Klansmen riding boldly in broad daylight.

"Hurry!" she exclaimed to David and Laura. "Go out the back door and run home as fast as you can. Tell the sheriff the Ku Klux Klan is paying me a social call."

"I won't leave you here alone with them," David insisted. "They're crazy. My pa says they'd kill at the drop of a hat. But what do they want with you?"

"They are crazy, indeed. Which is precisely why you both must leave. If you really want to help me, you'll fetch the sheriff, and you'll not waste a minute doing it!"

Valerie shoved them out the back door, hoping the Klansmen hadn't yet surrounded the schoolhouse. It seemed like an hour passed from the time she'd heard the horses' hooves to when the white-robed men burst into the schoolroom.

She was seated behind her desk as they approached her. "Well, gentlemen," she said coolly, "to what do I owe the pleasure of your company this afternoon?"

"You're stirrin' up trouble," the leader said, "tellin' folks not to listen to our message, tellin' folks we're crazy as bedbugs an' such. And I aim to see you stop it."

"Are you threatening me, Henry Cooper?"

He stood stock-still—amazed, she presumed, that she knew his identity.

"No threats necessary, ma'am. What we bring are promises: You stop bad-mouthin' us, an' we'll leave you alone."

She stood up slowly and rested the palms of her hands on the top of her desk. "And if I don't?"

Henry snickered quietly. "If you don't...." He glanced around the room at the shelves lined with books. At the blackboard.

At the neat rows of desks. "If you don't, you can kiss all this good-bye."

She'd expected him to threaten her, personally. Never in her wildest imaginings had she thought he'd destroy the schoolhouse! "Your own son is getting a fine education here in this building," she said, coming out from behind her desk to face him squarely. "Someday, Andy will grow up to be a fine man. He's a smart boy. He could go far in this world, provided you don't do something stupid, like interrupt his education to further your—your *mission*." She spat out the last word to show him her distaste for him and all that he stood for.

"You have a choice, Miss Carter: stop spreading lies about this organization, or *we'll stop you*."

"*For so is the will of God, that with well doing ye may put to silence the ignorance of foolish men,*'" she recited, boldly meeting the men's eyes peeking through the holes in their horrible hoods. "I will continue to do what I believe in my heart to be right."

"Mark my words," Henry said, his voice full of venom, "we will do what we must—"

"...to fulfill your mission. Yes, I recall your saying something similar the night all of you big, strong men overpowered one helpless woman and her child. Well, you mark *my* words: if anything happens to this schoolhouse, or to as much as one page of any book on these shelves, I'll know who was responsible. I'll gladly testify—"

"Won't be necessary," came the voice of Josh Kent. "Law says when an officer of the court witnesses a violation, he can make an arrest on the spot. No witnesses required."

Valerie smiled. Josh was becoming her knight in shining armor, one heroic deed at a time.

The sound of his pistol being cocked cracked the silence of the room. In seconds, rifles, shotguns, and handguns echoed the sound. "I said it before, and I'll say it again: take note of where the barrel of *my* gun is aimed, Cooper. And just for the benefit of you boys in the back…that would be dead center in his hard, little heart. And unless you believe his heart is hard enough to stop a bullet, you oughtn't be standin' behind him thataway."

The eyes in the hoods' holes widened.

"One shot, and you're gonna have to call a special meeting to appoint yourselves a new boss."

Henry lowered his weapon and gestured for his men to do the same. "By gosh, Henry," one said, "this is gettin' to be a bad habit. I ain't a-goin' to be part of terrorizin' women an' children no more." With that, he turned on his heel and stomped out of the schoolhouse. Two more Klansmen followed close behind.

Henry whirled around and shouted after them, "Go on and run off, ya yellow-bellied cowards. The rest of us will protect the white race in spite of you!"

"Protect it from *what?*" Josh demanded. "Seems to me the only thing threatenin' us is dunderheads like you. Now, why don't you climb back up on your ponies out there and ride on home? Have yourself a nice, hot supper and a good night's sleep. With any luck, you'll wake up tomorrow with the sense God gave you and put all this nonsense behind you, once an' for all."

When nobody moved, Josh took a step forward. "Go on, now, git. All o' you, before I get mad an' do somethin' ornery."

The four men still standing behind Henry filed out of the schoolhouse, one by one. Two of them added their hoods and robes to the pile of those left behind by the first men to flee, leaving only Henry and two devotees to ride away in full costume.

"You ain't seen the last of us," Henry hollered as he rode off. "Not by a long shot."

"It's gonna take a long shot," Josh hollered back, stuffing his gun into its holster, "'cause you ain't got the courage to do anything out in the open, up close."

When they were gone at last, he draped an arm over Valerie's shoulders. "Little Missy, ain't there *anythin'* you're afraid of?"

His protective embrace opened the floodgates, and she let herself lean against his strong chest. "There, there," he soothed, stroking her hair. "It's over...at least for now."

"I feel responsible somehow."

Valerie frowned. "Why, Paul, that's just silly, and you know it," she said matter-of-factly. "You were nowhere nearby on either occasion. Why would you feel responsible?"

Paul had to give her that. Even on his fastest horse, he couldn't get from his farm to the schoolhouse in less than thirty minutes.

He couldn't remember feeling more frustrated. The woman he loved had twice been in jeopardy, and there hadn't been a blessed thing he could do but listen afterward, helplessly, as the sheriff bragged about what a stouthearted little lady Valerie was to go head-to-head with the bad guys the way she had.

Again, he found himself wishing he'd proposed to her back in December.

But he didn't wish to have her as his wife simply to protect her. He wanted her because—*because I love her!* he admitted for the hundredth time.

And this time, he was determined to do something about it. Which was why he'd saddled up his big, black mare and made her gallop at full tilt all the way to Valerie's house.

She'd been peeling peaches when he arrived. Now, after several minutes in her tiny kitchen, watching her peek into the big, bubbling kettle to check on her canning jars and lids, he felt his impatience mounting. He wanted to take her in his arms and ask her to marry him.

She looked pretty, as usual. The white apron she wore ruffled daintily around her shoulders, and she'd wrapped her flowing hair with a red bandanna, accenting her cherubic face.

Paul didn't know which was sweeter—the sugary peaches boiling on the stove or the woman who'd smiled and invited him inside.

After pouring him a glass of lemonade, Valerie put him to work ladling fruit into the wide-mouthed jars that covered her kitchen table. When he splattered juice on his trousers, she stood behind him and wrapped a linen towel around his waist. Having her arms around him felt as normal and natural as breathing, and Paul was sorry when she finally tied the knot at the small of his back and stepped up to the stove to stir the peach pot.

He decided to leap right into the subject of her second altercation with the Klan. "If you were a cat," he said sullenly, "you'd already have used up two of your nine lives."

Valerie giggled. "Well, then, I guess we're both glad that I'm not a feline, aren't we?"

"It's no laughing matter, Valerie. You've got to stop barging into situations that put you in danger."

She put her hands on her hips and narrowed her big green eyes at him. "Now, you wait just a minute, Paul Collins. Let me remind you that on neither occasion did I voluntarily enter into a confrontation with the Klan. I appreciate your concern, but I resent your talking to me as if I were your responsibility. You're not my husband, and—"

"Yet," Paul interrupted her.

Valerie blinked absently at him. "What?"

"I'm not your husband. At least, not yet."

She busied herself rearranging jars on the tabletop.

"I'd have asked you to marry me months ago if I'd known you'd go and get yourself into trouble at every turn."

Her hands stopped in midair above the table, and a tiny grin formed on her face. "Trouble? That's all it would have taken to get you to pop the question?"

He put down the ladle and met her gaze. "Are you saying that if I'd asked you to marry me, you'd have said—"

"Miss Carter!" called a tiny voice from the other side of the door, "Mama sent me over to borrow a cup of sugar."

"Come in, Florence," Valerie said, holding the door open for the little girl. "What's your mother up to today? Cobbler? Cake?"

Florence giggled. "She sent Pa to pick a basketful of grapes, and now she's a sugar-cup short of turnin' 'em into jam. She said to promise you a jar in return for the loan."

Valerie handed the child a large, sturdy mug filled with sugar. "You tell your mother it's a deal!"

Florence eyed the table covered in jars. "What're *you* makin'?" she asked.

"Peach preserves," Valerie said, buttering a thick slice of bread, then slathering it with a spoonful of preserves. "Here," she said, handing it to Florence. "Let me know if it's any good."

At the little girl's bright-eyed grin when she took a bite, Valerie handed her a jar to take home to her mother.

Seeing Florence made Paul remember his own children, and he prepared to head home, albeit a little reluctantly. As Valerie was packing up three jars of preserves for him to take home, he whispered into her hair, "We're going to finish that conversation, Miss Carter. And soon. You can count on it." With a wink and a grin, he waved a quick good-bye and left her standing there, alone, in her kitchen.

She thought about his parting comment long after all the peaches had been canned and the jars had been stored away in her tiny root cellar. Long after the canning utensils had been washed up and put away.

Just before sunset, she settled into the rickety, old rocker on the front porch to watch the sky turn orange and purple. Thanks to Paul, she felt like the wealthiest woman in Freeland. She couldn't name another lady in town who had *three* rocking chairs! Later, as the night sky twinkled with stars and fireflies, Valerie decided that if Paul had been serious—if he did really plan to propose to her— she'd have no choice but to say yes. And she'd say it loudly and quickly, so he wouldn't have even a moment to change his mind.

The scene in the church basement on Christmas Day unfolded behind her closed eyelids: three loving children and one loving man, all of them needing her every bit as much as she needed them.

The Lord had blessed her, for sure. But how long would He test her patience? How long until Paul would say the words she longed to hear? *Paul, Paul, why persecutest thou me?* Valerie thought, smiling wryly.

At long last, graduation day arrived. Valerie had sent invitations to everyone in town and hoped they'd all show up for the school's first real ceremony.

She decorated the schoolhouse with red, white, and blue banners in honor of the occasion. It was such a lovely day that she dragged out every bench, chair, crate, and box from the school-house and stood them in neat, orderly rows in the shade of the oak grove behind the school. David Garvey and Laura Harper had prepared short speeches to inspire and encourage the classmates they were leaving behind, and the younger children had written a play in honor of the graduates.

Songs had been rehearsed.

Awards had been printed.

Diplomas had been penned.

In less than an hour, Valerie would stand at the lectern and introduce two students who had come to mean so much to her during her first year as Freeland's schoolmarm. For their sakes, she hoped every seat would be filled.

She'd made a huge bowl of fruit punch and baked two cakes and six pies. Greta had volunteered a smoked ham, and Mrs. Gemmill had promised to bring her famous baked beans.

At last, the long-awaited moment arrived. David, wearing a stiff-collared shirt and a neat, black bow tie, sat straight and tall in one of the two ladder-back chairs that faced the audience. Laura, her hair tied up in a pretty, pink bow, wore a lovely white dress and matching pinafore. As Valerie, in her white-trimmed navy frock, took her place behind the podium, Rev. Gemmill cleared his throat and coughed to command silence from the crowd.

"Ladies and gentlemen," Valerie began, "I am so pleased to see how many of you turned out to share in this wonderful day with David Garvey and Laura Harper. They have worked hard to reach this goal, and I'm sure it means a lot to them to know they have your support and congratulations.

"David will be leaving us soon, as some of you know. He'll be gone for several years, and we'll miss him greatly."

David blushed when she smiled approvingly at him.

"When he returns, we'll most likely present him with a shingle that reads, 'David Garvey, Doctor of Veterinary Medicine.'"

She waited for the applause to fade away before continuing.

"Laura Harper, soon to become Mrs. Jonathan Hall, will remain here in Freeland, I'm happy to say. She's agreed to be my teaching assistant, so your children will have the benefit of not one, but two teachers!"

Again, she waited for the applause to fade before going on.

"Soon, each and every child in our little school will sit where David and Laura are seated now," Valerie continued. "I'm certain of that. We're fortunate to have such dedicated and hardworking young people among us who will someday contribute to our little community in the same way their parents and grandparents before them did.

"They'll achieve that end because of you," she said, gesturing toward the audience. "You built this school. You hired me. You see to it that your children come here every day. Your unfailing dedication as parents, relatives, neighbors, and friends is directly responsible for Freeland's promising future."

She reached under the podium and retrieved two black album-like booklets, then held them up for all to see.

"In these leather bindings," she said, "is the official proof that this young man and this young woman have completed their primary educations. But the true proof of all they've learned is in the eyes and minds and hearts of David and Laura.

"David Allen Garvey," she said, slowly and deliberately, "will you please join me at the podium?"

David walked stiff-legged across the lawn and came to stand beside Valerie, grinning and blushing like a small boy, even though he was head and shoulders taller than his teacher and outweighed her by at least fifty pounds.

"This is your diploma, David," she said, placing it in his outstretched hands. "I am so very proud of you!"

She hugged him and blinked back tears of joy, then said, "Laura Ann Harper, it's your turn...."

Laura tiptoed gracefully toward the stand and, looking down, smiled happily.

"You've earned this," Valerie said, handing the girl her diploma. "I'm proud of you, too."

Laura gave Valerie a tight hug. "Thank you, Miss Carter," she said. "I couldn't have done it without you." Then, she held her diploma high in the air and squealed with girlish delight.

Paul had taken a seat in the last row, though he'd arrived early enough to sit up front. His children, preferring to sit with their friends, were clustered in the middle rows, where they could whisper and giggle without disturbing the adults around them.

He'd sat back there so he could watch Valerie.

When she'd taken her place at the lectern, he'd feared his face would crack from the width of his proud smile. She looked lovely in her feminine dress; her thick, chestnut-colored hair refused to stay pinned in the proper schoolmarm's bun. She was so at ease in front of these people—smiling and meeting their eyes, gesturing with her delicate little hands, and adding emphasis to various statements now and then with a nod of her head.

Her sweet voice, as clear and crisp as the blue sky above, had carried her message of congratulations to everyone present. And her pride in David and Laura's accomplishments had shone brightly in her big, green eyes. Even from way in the back, Paul could see the soft curve of her long eyelashes.

During Valerie's speech, she'd met his eyes once and had sent him a smile so glorious that he'd thought his heart would burst with love. She was so many wonderful things all wrapped up in one tidy package—strength and warmth, intelligence and grace, beauty and love. And if he had his way today, he'd add another adjective to the list: his.

Chapter Ten

Valerie applauded the new graduates, and the rest of the townsfolk joined her.

While neighbors and relatives congratulated David and Laura, Valerie waved at Paul. Grinning, she half ran to join him at the back of the crowd. He'd walked across the little bridge above Licking Creek that separated the school yard from the road and was standing beneath the maple where they'd shared many sweet conversations. Valerie was glad he'd chosen this place, far from the gleeful crowd, where they'd be able to share a precious moment of privacy.

When Valerie had a little more than ten feet to go before she would grasp Paul's warm, welcoming hand, she froze. Her wide, loving smile of greeting faded instantly, replaced by a mask of disbelief and terror.

Paul had no time to register her fright. He was still wearing that wide, welcoming grin when the dull thud of the club connected with his skull.

Valerie opened her mouth to scream for help, but two white-hooded men rushed at her from either side. One clamped a huge, sweaty hand over her mouth, rendering her silent; the other held her arms. A third man suddenly joined them and jammed a dirty rag in her mouth. As Valerie squealed and struggled to free herself, she saw Paul drop limply to the ground.

And then, helpless to overpower her oppressors, Valerie watched the bright afternoon turn dark as the men yanked a burlap sack over her head.

Her feet, shuffling and scraping as she tried to escape, made no sound on the soft, grassy lawn.

Her screams, muffled by the gag, went unheard.

Then, Valerie felt herself be hoisted over one man's shoulder, carried away like a helpless kitten, and deposited none too gently into the back of a wagon that was filled with what felt like hay.

The ride was long and hard. She tried to pay attention to the noises she heard as they bumped along. Cows mooing. Horses whinnying. Crickets chirping. Locusts buzzing. All so clear, so ordinary—yet not one told her where these men were taking her.

She didn't need a detective's mind to know *who* had taken her. Henry Cooper, no doubt, had ordered her abduction. But once he got her where he wanted her, what would he do with her? Would he torture her? Would he beat her and then hang her, as he had tried to do to Ardith Johnson? Or was the whole kidnapping merely a ruse to frighten her into succumbing to his demands to stop spreading negative reports about the Klan?

"*Ye shall not need to fight in this battle: set yourselves, stand ye still, and see the salvation of the LORD with you.*" Repeating 2 Chronicles 20:17 in her mind brought her a small measure of comfort. A very small measure.

Valerie searched her memory for more Bible passages that would help her remain strong, verses that would help her stand firm once the wagon stopped and her captors announced their demands.

Ephesians 2:5: "*By grace ye are saved.*" Psalm 25:2: "*O my God, I trust in thee:…let not mine enemies triumph over me.*" Proverbs 15:3:

"*The eyes of the* LORD *are in every place, beholding the evil and the good.*" Jonah 2:7: "*When my soul fainted within me I remembered the* LORD." Deuteronomy 20:1: "*Be not afraid of them: for the* LORD *thy God is with thee.*"

Valerie clung to that last one from Deuteronomy, repeating it over and over in her mind. It had a somewhat calming effect.

Until the wagon stopped.

Valerie wanted to trust the Lord to protect her, but she knew that no one had seen these men steal her away; they'd clubbed Paul and left him there, alone and unconscious. She hoped someone had found him by now and was tending his head injury.

She whispered a prayer for his safety and well-being: "'*Be not afraid of them: for the* LORD *thy God is with thee.*'" Then, she said it again with conviction as rough hands grabbed her and yanked her from the wagon. She was led over a grassy area and on to a patch of gravel that crunched beneath her feet for about three steps.

She was on solid ground now.

Hard and…smooth?

The air around her became suddenly chilly, and the pinholes of light that had been filtering in through the burlap bag went out.

The men's movements, their footsteps, and even their whispered commands echoed loudly.

We're in a cave! she realized, fighting to control her terror. *No one will ever find me—or hear me—in here…. "'Be not afraid of them…,'*" she prayed fervently, silently. "'*Be not be afraid….'*" She realized that if she let them see her fear, she might never get out of this mess alive.

"Take that thing off her head and let her loose."

Valerie recognized the voice as Henry Cooper's.

"But she'll know who we are," said another man.

"Not if you keep your hoods on," Henry barked.

Soon, blinking in the brightness of their torches, Valerie stood face-to-face with her abductors. She bit her lower lip to keep it from trembling.

"Not so brave now that you don't have your highfalutin sheriff around to protect you, are you?" Henry asked, his voice smug with hatred.

Valerie found herself unable to speak. What would she say? That she *was* brave? That she *didn't* wish Josh would show up?

"I warned you to keep your vile comments about the Klan to yourself. What's that old saying? *'Physician, heal thyself'*?" Henry laughed long and hard. "Let's put a twist on it, why don't we? Teacher, listen and learn. You taught the children to obey direct instructions but never learned the lesson for yourself."

"No one saw you kidnap me," Valerie said, finding her voice at last. "What sort of example can you set for the others who might oppose you if no one knows what you've done? You can't very well volunteer this information. If you could do that, you wouldn't need to hide your identities behind those horrible masks."

The eyes behind the gaping holes in Henry's hood grew increasingly fierce and angry. "That's where you're wrong, missy. We have ways of spreading the word. Folks'll know what happened to you, all right. And they'll know *why*."

She'd never been this afraid for her life. Not when she'd gotten lost in downtown Richmond at the age of six. Not when she'd wandered away from a family picnic and had had to climb a tree to escape a black bear. Not even on the day the Yankees had set fire to Carter Hall. Those things had been accidents. Matters of happenstance. Events that had occurred according to no particular plan to harm Valerie Carter. But these men had a deliberate plan, and she was at the center of it.

"How can I be such a great threat to your mission?" she asked, suddenly angry. "I'm one voice. One woman. What damage can I do to you or your movement?"

Henry gave a short, nervous laugh. "In better days, I'd have agreed with you, little lady. But, unfortunately, you've got more power than you know. Some of my men have gone soft, thanks to your sorry little message about equality and freedom. And some of 'em believe that nonsense you've been quoting from the Constitution.

"We've lost over a dozen members since you started your anti-Klan campaign. People had been falling into line left and right, with hardly a backward glance. But now…." Henry shrugged and shook his head. "Seems they don't want to offend Uppity Miss Carter. Maybe they're afraid you'll quit teachin' their young'uns, afraid they'll never find another teacher as gullible as you to work as hard as you do for the tiny salary they give you."

Henry was angry, all right—angry at her powers of persuasion, at the number of friends she'd made in town. But if she'd persuaded any of them, it had been only because she'd quoted what God and the country's forefathers had deemed right and true, and they'd agreed!

"What are you afraid of, Henry? That some Negro or Jew will stand beside you and, by contrast, make your ignorance shine like a beacon for all to see?"

With the back of his hand, Henry slapped her. Hard.

Two of his followers stepped forward, as if to defend her.

"Get back!" Henry barked. "Or there'll be some of that for you, too!"

The pair hemmed and hawed, uncertain whether or not to obey.

"Put that rag back in her mouth. I've heard about enough from her for one day."

While his followers hunted up the rag to do Henry's bidding, Valerie filled the cool, quiet air with questions: "How did you get so filled with hate, Henry? What happened to turn your soul black and your heart to ice? What makes you so sure your message is good and holy?"

The other men looked at him hard, as though, suddenly, merely hearing Valerie's simple questions, they were wondering the same things.

"Get that rag in her mouth, I tell you!" Henry growled. "If I have to do it myself, I swear I'll stuff it so far down her throat, she'll choke before we have the chance to hang her."

"Hang her!" one of the men shouted. "You never said anything about hanging her. We were only supposed to bring her here to teach her a lesson about being quiet and obedient. I told you the night you hung Abel, I'd not take part in any more killings, or in the beating of white women, Henry."

"I'm with you," another man said. "Killin' niggers ain't worth goin' to prison or swingin' at the end of a rope."

"It *is* worth your lives," Henry shouted, his crazed voice echoing through the hollow interior of the cave. "If you're not willing to give your life, you don't belong in this army. If you're not willing to lie down and die for the cause, you don't deserve to call yourself a Klansman."

"Maybe you're right," said the first man.

"Not maybe—definitely," agreed the second.

The pair of them marched out of the cave, tossing down their robes and hoods.

That left Henry only three followers.

"Get out there and make sure they understand what'll happen if they don't respect the oaths they took when they joined up," he told two of them. "The fires and the noose can be set up just as easily where they live, y'know."

The men hurried outside to deliver the warning. During the next hour, the soft shuffling of feet, an occasional clearing of a throat, and several deep sighs were the only sounds in the damp, chilly cave. But the Klansmen never returned.

"No matter," Henry said. "We can summon up as many reinforcements as we need that fast," he added, snapping his fingers, "by sending a one-line telegram to Tennessee. Those lily-livered cowards are of no worry to us. All of 'em know where they stand... and where they'll fall if they cross us." He glared at Valerie. "If we're feelin' real Christian in the mornin', we might just come back with some food for you."

Then, with a wave of his hand, he bid his last soldier follow him out of the cave. They took their lanterns with them, removing all light and the warmth, as well.

Valerie slid down the cold, rock wall and huddled against a boulder, shivering. The man who'd put the gag in her mouth hadn't done a very thorough job. She wondered if it had been an accident, or if he'd been reexamining his conscience, too.

Carefully, so she could drag it back between her teeth should the men reappear, Valerie deposited it on the ground beside her.

Goosebumps pimpled her forearms. Her heart thumped wildly. "Our Father, who art in heaven," she prayed through her tears, "deliver me from evil...."

When Paul came to, he was looking up into the worried faces of his children and the sheriff. "What in tarnation happened to you?" Josh asked him. "You've got a knot on the back of y   .ull the size of a goose egg."

Paul winced with pain as he tried to sit up. Last thing he knew, he'd been walking toward Valerie in the school yard. "How'd I get here?" he wanted to know, squinting around at the interior of Doc Gifford's office.

"Your young'uns came and got me," Josh said, "and I fetched the doc once I saw how far out of it you were."

"How long have I been out?"

Doc opened his pocket watch. "Nearly two hours. Think you can stand up?"

It took Josh and Doc supporting him, but Paul managed to get to his feet. He stood there for a moment, wobbling on limp legs. Suddenly, he remembered the last thing he'd seen before everything had gone black—Valerie's terrified, wide-eyed expression. She'd seen something she'd tried to warn him about. But what? "Where's Valerie?"

Doc shrugged. "Dunno. Nobody's seen her since the graduation ended."

Paul struggled to free himself from his friends' grasp. "She's not at the schoolhouse?"

"Nope," said Josh.

"What about her house? Has anyone looked there?"

Josh only frowned. "Now, why didn't I think of that?" he said, sarcasm ringing in his voice. "Give me a little credit, Paul—that was the first place I looked!"

"But—"

"Sit down, Paul, before you fall down," Doc said. "Say something comforting to these children of yours. They've been hovering over you, worried sick, since they found you under the oak tree in the school yard."

Paul slumped onto the cot against Doc's office wall and looked into their faces to see the same terrified expressions they'd worn when they'd seen the Yankee bullet rip through their mother. Before he said another word, he had to reassure them that he was all right. "C'mere, you guys," he said, holding out his arms. The children piled into them and snuggled close. "Your old pa is fine," he said. "I've got me a headache the size of a watermelon, but I'm just fine." He kissed their foreheads. "Now, what say you take this nickel here," he said, digging in his pocket, "and run over to Greta's. See if she'll fix me up with a nice, cold bottle of root beer to make my headache better."

The children scrambled to their feet and headed for the door, happy to be doing something—anything—to help their father feel like his old self again. When the door banged shut behind them, Paul met Josh's gaze.

"She hasn't been seen or heard from since the graduation?"

"That's right, Paul," Josh said. "I've been all up and down Main Street, askin' about her." He shook his head and shrugged. "Nothin'."

Paul held his head in his hands. He'd been on the verge of asking her to marry him. Right on the cusp of making her his for the rest of his life...if he was lucky. "Well," he said, running his hands through his hair, "you must have some idea what happened. Tell me what you think."

Josh and Doc exchanged worried glances. "Might not be a good idea, Paul. We know you're kinda...soft on Valerie."

Paul shook his head. "Soft? I'm crazy in love with her, man! If I hadn't taken this hit on the noggin, she'd have this ring on her finger by now!" Paul reached into his shirt pocket. Slowly, tenderly, he unfolded a red bandanna. Inside, a simple gold band glittered in the lamplight.

"Well, I'll be," Doc said.

"Would ya look at that," Josh added.

"I have a right to know what your suspicions are," Paul insisted.

"Do ya reckon she'd a'said yes?" Josh asked, a slight smile slanting his mouth.

Paul nodded. "Yes, I think she would have. At least, I surely hope she would have...."

Again, Josh and the doctor traded serious glances. "Guess we might as well tell him the worst of it," Doc said.

Josh took a deep breath, sat down on Doc's rolling stool, and leaned his elbows on his knees. "It's like this, Paul.... We found footprints in the flower garden near her porch. Big prints. Lots of 'em. And the tracks of at least a dozen horses. Shod horses, mind you." He stared at the floor between his booted feet, as if telling Paul that the rest of it hurt him as much as he knew it would hurt Paul. "Somebody was watchin' her, Paul. On more'n one occasion, from the looks of things."

"The Klan...."

Doc nodded. "Who else?"

"We followed their trail. Led us right to the hitchin' post beside the school. And the wagon tracks...." Josh frowned and stared out the window. "The wagon tracks lead up into the hills."

Paul stood and headed for the door. "Well, what are we waiting for? Let's go and find her!"

"Sit down, you fool man," Doc said. "There's more. And you're not going to like this last piece of news one little bit."

Paul's head swam and his legs felt rubbery. He did as Doc suggested.

"We followed the wagon tracks into the hills. But that's where they end. We can't be sure which direction they headed in once they parked the wagon."

Paul glanced out the window to see that the afternoon light was already beginning to fade. Again, he held his head in his hands. Not one living soul had ever seen him cry. Not when the heart attack had taken his father. Not when he'd received the news about his brother. Not even when a bullet had ripped through Rita. But now....

Josh and Doc shuffled from one foot to the other, not knowing what to say or do to comfort their friend.

Valerie could only hope the quiet scraping noises she heard weren't the sounds of a bear. Or a snake, on its way home to seek warmth from the cool, night air. In the light of day, she had no fear of such things. But then, there was little to fear from things one could see....

Henry had left enough slack in her bindings to allow her to move her hands. The gag she'd removed from her mouth still rested on the ground beside her.

She almost physically swallowed her fear and noticed, dismally, that even the simple act of swallowing had grown difficult. That puzzled her, until she recalled a newspaper story she'd read about savage Indians out West who tortured settlers by binding them with damp strips of rawhide. As the strips dried, they tightened, strangling their victims...slowly.

Henry had tethered Valerie in just that way once his loyal devotees had fled the cave. He'd bound her wrists and ankles, then looped the strip twice around her neck.

Already, she felt its deadly strands drying, tightening, cutting off her breath.

Stay calm, she told herself. *Think!*

Was that water she heard dripping in the distance? She strained to identify the sound coming from somewhere deep in the belly of the cave, then started crawling toward it. If she could find the steady water supply, she believed, she might be able to lie beneath it so that it would drip on the bindings and keep them damp.

Scraping across the rock-hard cave floor, she tore her dress and stockings, and knew she was bloodying her knees, too. One foot landed with a *splat* in a tiny puddle. "Praise the Lord—water!" Leaning against the wall, she allowed the cold liquid to drip onto her bindings one icy plop at a time.

Sleepiness threatened to overtake her, and she knew she needed to fight it. If she gave in to slumber, she might slump to the floor, out of the water's path. And if that happened, the rawhide ties would dry as she slept, and….

Valerie thought of Paul. About his hint at marriage. She'd gladly tie herself to him for a lifetime, if he asked.

Her mother had always said, "Love is the tie that binds." Valerie grinned sardonically. *Mother's words have a totally new meaning today*, she thought.

Her eyelids drooped as drowsiness set in.

Suddenly, a high-pitched squeak echoed through the cave. Then came more of the scraping sounds she'd heard earlier, followed by a flurry of flapping wings.

Bats! she realized, ducking instinctively.

But she was in no danger from the bats, she knew. The only peril she faced was in the form of rawhide strips.

She prayed the Twenty-third Psalm. She said the Lord's Prayer. She sang "Amazing Grace" with more conviction than ever before. She counted all the way to three thousand five hundred and sixty-six.

She also recited the Gettysburg Address. She'd clipped it out of the newspaper because it had moved her, and she'd memorized it for the same reason. If she'd known little things like this could help pass the time during a kidnapping, she'd have memorized the Preamble to the Constitution. The Bill of Rights. The *entire* Constitution, for heaven's sake!

She hadn't eaten since morning, and the hunger pangs were becoming more pronounced.

Why doesn't someone come? she ranted silently. Even the Klansmen would be a welcome sight at this point.

Well, almost.

At least she'd know once and for all where she stood with them. Whether or not they planned to hang her. Or turn her loose. Or beat her the way they'd beaten Ardith. Or....

The possibilities frightened Valerie even more than the actual threats had. She said a prayer that when the time came, she'd be strong and brave, that she wouldn't give them the satisfaction of knowing how terrified she was.

She said another prayer for Paul's safety.

And, despite her best efforts to avoid it, she drifted off to sleep.

Chapter Eleven

Valerie slept so deeply that she was temporarily oblivious to the fact that her bed was made of stone.

Her dream took her back in time—took her south to the wide, warm plantation known throughout Virginia, Carter Hall.

But the beauty of the vast landscape burned up before her very eyes, and, as she dreamed, Valerie could feel the fire's residual heat. She stood stock-still in the ashes and listened as a soft wind sighed through the row of pines lining the farm road; listened as it echoed across the mansion's foundation, where the housekeeper, Marjorie, had recently dusted the polished wood floors for her mother's annual Christmas ball.

There, where bright fires had once licked pot bottoms in the keeping room's hearth, the crackling power of the Yankees' torches burned instead.

Valerie cried softly, almost silently, as she stepped through the remains of Carter Hall, picking her way through the debris in search of something—anything—she could take with her, something to remind her of this house and the people who had called it home.

Smoke plumes rose up from the sooty earth and threatened to choke the life from her, just as the blaze had choked the life from Carter Hall.

She was grasping her throat when she awoke. Grasping her throat and sobbing. Immediately, she realized that her leather bindings had begun to dry as she'd slept. She patted the cave floor in search of the puddle....

Finding it, she sighed with relief, understanding fully why the treasured liquid had so often been called "life sustaining."

As she lay back and let the droplets fall, one by one, onto the ties that bound her, Valerie shivered and recalled her dream.

She supposed she'd been reliving that awful day from her past because the events of it had terrified her so much. They had changed the entire course of her life, just as the events of these past two days and nights had.

Perhaps the nightmare had returned here, in the chilling bleakness of the cave that was her prison, because it offered the promise of warmth, even if the memories were cold.

Valerie remembered stepping into an icebox with her father once. A train had pulled in at the station near the docks in Norfolk, Virginia, and she'd stood aside as her father inspected a shipment of fruits and vegetables from the Caribbean. Huge chunks of sparkling, translucent ice had lined the walls of the boxcar, and the floors, wet with puddles, had stunk of remnants of shipments past—fish, meat, poultry, and vegetables from faraway lands. Being in that cold place had reminded the young Valerie of the evening fogs that so often blanketed the streambed near Carter Hall, though the air in the boxcar hadn't clung to her in the same seemingly mystical way.

Being imprisoned in this cave made her think of that boxcar, though the frigid temperature had no man-made cause; it was from the powerful hand of Mother Nature.

Valerie blinked into the semidarkness and welcomed this second morning of life. Obviously, since the Klansmen hadn't returned as Henry had threatened they would, it seemed they intended to leave her in the cave to starve to death—that is, if she didn't choke first.

She shook her head to clear the frightening thoughts from her mind.

Well, she had no intention of just lying down to die. She'd fight to live, even if it killed her!

It took Valerie the better part of an hour to struggle to her feet. Once she'd achieved a fully upright position, she leaned for a moment against the chilly cave wall to secure her footing and catch her ragged breath.

First, she canvassed the cave floor, which seemed to span endlessly between her and the cave's entrance. The ground was smooth and flat. She took a few unsteady jumps forward, then stopped, deciding instead to take tiny, shuffling steps like the Oriental girls on the Richmond docks, who dressed in kimonos and wore tiny thongs on their feet. It was slow going at first, especially since she was forced to consider that without her arms free to protect her, a fall would probably leave her unconscious until....

Valerie swallowed, feeling the pressure of the leather strip around her neck. Her energy, she believed, would be far better spent planning her survival.

Sunshine brightened the sky outside the mouth of the cave, and with the light came warmth—warmth that would dry her damp skirt and petticoat, warmth that would dry the leather, too....

She didn't have a moment to waste.

She surveyed what lay beyond the cave and saw, perhaps a hundred yards from where she was standing, a field of white daisies. She hobbled toward it. On the other side, she hoped, there'd be a road. A well-travelled road.

She moved forward, glancing back once she reached the edge of the field. From here, the entrance to the cave looked like a yawning giant. Should she return to what she knew for certain, or head for parts unknown?

Either way, whether out here in the bright sunshine or inside the gloomy cave, the leather would surely dry and tighten and....

Valerie dropped to her knees and prayed, "'Be not afraid...: for the LORD thy God is with thee....'"

When she looked up, the horizon, even with all its uncertainty and potential pitfalls and dangers, looked far more welcoming than the ugly, black mouth of the cave. She was tired. Every muscle and joint ached. She was hungry and thirsty. And frightened.

All she wanted was to lie down and sleep, to put this miserable moment in time far, far behind her.

She'd rest here, surrounded by the lovely white blossoms, but for a moment....

Paul, Josh, and Doc led the search party.

The moment the men of Freeland heard what had likely happened to their beloved schoolmarm, twenty-three of the town's strapping gents had picked up rifles, shotguns, and sidearms to join the hunt. They'd been at it since the night of the town's first graduation ceremony. Since then, they'd seen two sunrises.

They'd combed every square inch of the roadside where Josh had seen the last of the wagon wheel's tracks. With the help of two saplings growing alongside the road, Paul pulled himself up an embankment. From his new vantage point, he was able to survey the countryside in all directions.

Shielding his eyes from the sun with one hand, he scanned the horizon, praying as he did for some sign that the Klansmen had brought Valerie in this direction.

Almost immediately, he noticed a broken branch in the brush up ahead. And beyond that, he saw a fallen, rotting limb that was crushed—possibly by a large, booted foot. "Over here," he called to his fellow searchers. "I think I've spotted something."

Hurrying ahead, he looked for other signs and clues that humans had been where usually only wild things tread. And he found them: broken branches. Crumpled underbrush. A smashed wildflower. A footprint in a patch of caked mud. The evidence was everywhere, and he hooted with glee.

"Look at that," Josh said, pointing at the cave. It seemed they all saw it at once, and they ran full tilt toward it, into it, only to find an empty, hollow, echoing chasm.

"She's been here," Josh announced, putting one knee on the floor as he bent to pick up a grimy rag. "Get a whiff of that," he said, handing it to Paul.

Taking it, Paul inhaled, eyes closed, then whispered, "Roses...."

"There's only one way she could have gone," Doc said, standing in the opening and clutching his black medical bag, "and that's straight ahead." He held up a scrap of leather. "We've got to assume she's been tied, so I don't suppose she could have gone very far. I'll bet if we head in that direction," he added, gesturing ahead, "we'll catch up to her in no time."

"She could have been moving all night," Josh said. "No telling how far she'd get in that time."

"She mighta got turned round in der voods," DeWitt put in.

"Not if her wrists and ankles are bound," Paul said, marching up the gradual incline that led toward the field of daisies. "I was right," he said almost immediately. "You can see that she's been taking small steps...."

The others gathered around to have a look at the tracks Valerie had made.

Hope filled Paul's heart, and he had to restrain himself from running ahead. "She's too smart to have tried moving through here in the dark," he said. "She'd have waited for first light. If she started out this morning, she can't be more than a few hundred yards ahead of us...."

The men fanned out and moved forward, not letting an inch of ground go uncovered. In less than thirty minutes, Josh whistled to get the others' attention. Once he had it, he pointed at the deep-blue mound just beyond the clearing.

Paul's eyes followed Josh's directions until he, too, saw the mound.

Blue.

Deep, dark blue.

Like the dress Valerie had worn to the graduation ceremony.

No, not *like* the dress she'd worn—it *was* the dress she'd worn....

Paul raced toward the small mound, not stopping until he was beside her. "Valerie, honey," he panted, pulling her onto his lap, "are you all right?"

Woozily, she grinned up at him. "Well, it sure would be nice to scratch this itch on my nose. Can't reach it, though," she said, giggling, "'cause I seem to be all tied up at the moment."

Paul smiled. Only Valerie could use humor in such a moment. Gently, Paul cut the binding from around her neck, followed by the ropes that bound her wrists and ankles. But when she was finally freed from her restraints, much to his surprise, she didn't scratch her nose at all. Instead, she threw her arms around his and kissed his cheek.

"My, but you're a sight for sore eyes, Paul Collins! Now, would you mind helping me up?" she said. "I dearly love daisies—they're my all-time favorite flower, as a matter of fact—but I don't relish the prospect of spending another moment facedown in a field of them!"

The search party held back and gave the two a few moments of privacy before joining them. When they finally did, Josh folded his arms over his broad chest and asked, "What's the story here?"

Valerie sighed. "Well, Josh, I hope you have plenty of time, because it's a long, strange story."

And then she fainted.

The Klan's hold on Freeland wasn't as tight as everyone had imagined. In fact, the stranger who had come to town to solicit recruits for the movement left town on the same day that Henry Cooper was arrested for abducting Valerie. "We have too much important work to do," the man whispered between the steel bars on the window of Henry's jail cell, "not to leave any witnesses." He adjusted the cinch on his saddle as he concluded, "We trusted you with this regiment, Cooper, but you proved yourself unworthy of that trust. You were sloppy, and it cost us. We'll continue on as planned, and the movement will grow stronger without the likes of you."

Because Valerie couldn't bear to see the Cooper family lose their only means of support, she didn't press charges against Henry. Neither did she name any of the other Klansmen who had abducted her. In place of gratitude, Henry met her with the same hate-filled eyes as before. Somewhere within him beat the heart of the old Henry Cooper—the Henry who, before his involvement with the Klan, had been a kinder, gentler man. Still, his heart was ashamed of what the new Henry had done and somehow talked him into selling the farm. No one knew where the family would go.

No one much cared.

The last anyone saw of the Coopers, they were heading north as the wedding march for the newly graduated Laura Harper began. Valerie missed seeing the procession down the center aisle because she couldn't make herself go inside the church. Instead, she stood on the porch, her eyes fixed on Andy Cooper's sad face. She watched it grow smaller as the distance between him and the only home he'd ever known grew. Just before he disappeared from view, he raised his hand and waved a final good-bye. "I'm sorry," he mouthed silently. "I'm so sorry...."

Valerie knew she'd see that pained expression in her mind's eye for a long, long time.

Paul stepped outside in time to see what she'd seen. "What are you doing out here all by yourself?" he whispered, cupping her elbow. "You're missing the whole wedding."

Once she'd settled beside him in the pew, he held her hand and stared straight ahead, pretending not to notice the tears that were rolling down her cheeks. Her tears weren't caused by the emotional nature of a wedding ceremony, as those of many other women were. No, Valerie's tears were for Andy Cooper.

Paul gave her hand a little squeeze. He'd made few commitments in his life but took them very seriously. Now, he made a new commitment—he promised himself he'd do everything humanly possible to make sure Valerie would never have cause to cry again. That was one promise he aimed to keep.

He'd discussed his hopes of marrying Valerie with the children as recently as the night before, and they'd seemed as excited and pleased about the plan as Paul himself. *No time like the present,* he thought.

Rev. Gemmill's voice droned on as he read from the book of Genesis. Paul leaned closer to Valerie and said softly in her ear, "Marry me."

For a moment, he suspected that she hadn't heard him, for she continued to stare straight ahead. Blinking. Silent.

"Did you hear me?"

He watched her smile and nod, then felt her give his hand a little squeeze.

"Is that a yes?"

She nodded again and gave his hand another little squeeze.

"Look at me when you say it, then."

When she did, her green eyes brimmed with unshed tears. This time, he knew, they were tears of joy.

"Yes," she whispered.

"Yes, what?" he teased.

"Yes, I'll marry you."

"Shhh!" scolded Mrs. Potter, who was seated behind them. She rapped Paul's shoulder with her folded Spanish lace fan.

Paul turned around and said to the older woman, "I asked her to marry me, and she said yes!"

"Well, it's high time," Mrs. Potter whispered. "Now, face the front, young man, before I tan your hide like I used to when you were a naughty boy."

Paul's grin broadened. "Yes'm."

"Did you hear that?" Tricia asked her older brother. "Right in the middle of everything, Pa asked Miss Carter to marry him!"

Tyler grinned and rolled his eyes. "What're we s'posed to call her after *they* stand up there?"

Tricia hid her giggle behind a gloved hand.

Timmy tugged his big brother's sleeve. "What's all the whisperin' about?"

Tyler and Tricia exchanged amused glances. "Nothing," they said together. "Just a lot of grown-up wedding talk," Tricia explained quietly, patting her little brother's head.

At the sound of his daughter's voice, Paul met her eyes. *Why, she's positively beaming!* he thought. He glanced at Tyler and, finding the same expression on his son's face, felt his heart lurch with joy.

After the wedding, as Paul, Valerie, and the children waited their turn to congratulate the newlyweds in the receiving line, Timmy stood in the middle of the vestibule and proclaimed in a loud voice, "Miss Carter's gonna be my ma! Pa asked her to marry him, and she said yes!"

After a moment of stunned silence, much handshaking and cheek-kissing followed congratulatory wishes.

"Got a date set yet?" Josh Kent wanted to know.

"Planning to have more children right away?" asked Mrs. Potter.

And, from Doc, "We'll sure miss seein' your pretty face in town, Miss Valerie, when you move out to the farm."

"Vill you bring der young ones on der honeymoon?" Greta asked.

Paul blushed and Valerie giggled.

"What's a honeymoon?" Timmy asked, inspiring hearty laughter all around.

Valerie looked thrilled and overjoyed. But she said she did not want the attention that had been focused on their announcement to overshadow the happy couple. "This is Laura and Jonathan's day; there will be no more talk of any wedding but theirs!" she announced in her firmest schoolteacher's voice.

As part of the Fourth of July festivities every ear, Doc organized the Great Freeland Mule Race. For a dollar, anyone with a nag, pony, donkey, burro, or mule could register to run, and the winner received all the registration money. This year, a fancy Western saddle, donated by the new owner of the blacksmith shop, would be second prize. Third prize, as always, was a free supper for two at the Freelander Hotel.

Some of the men began betting on which entrant would come away with each prize. Josh's sturdy pony was the favorite, but Doc's keen eye chose Bertram Gardener's quarter horse to win.

Many proper and devout Christians clucked their tongues at the sinful practice of gambling. "*Having food and raiment let us be therewith content,*'" they said, quoting the Good Book. "'*...For the love of money is the root of all evil: which while some coveted after, they have erred from the faith, and pierced themselves through with many sorrows.*'"

Valerie, however, was not as quick to pass judgment. She believed her parents to have been the most God-fearing, God-loving individuals she'd ever known. Their weekly tithes and donations to charities had been generous. They'd taught her to trust the Lord and to pray to Him. Yet they hadn't condemned gambling outright.

Soon after her father, Lee, had assumed management of Carter Hall, a storm had threatened to ruin his promising tobacco crop. So, to encourage his hired hands to harvest the crops before the storm blew through, Lee had allowed the men to bet on who would pick the most tobacco in the least amount of time. By sundown, Willis had filled ninety-nine and one-half bushels with the broad, green leaves, and he'd gone home to his wife and children in their white cottage nearly ten dollars richer. He'd used the money to buy a rugged little wagon and a nag named Beulah.

The hands had worked harder that day than they'd ever worked; the tobacco crop had come in long before the storm had torn through the river valley. And the work had been done by happy, satisfied men. Never before had Lee seen them smile as they worked; never before had he heard such laughter.

So, Lee had made it a regular event. He'd raised their incentive to work hard as each crop was harvested, whether it be corn or cotton or tobacco, by promising to match the number of quarters in the sack with an equal number of his own. Fun and profit, the astute businessman had learned, were excellent incentives.

Valerie often heard the good Christians of Freeland denounce betting and gambling. But if her good and decent father, who'd worked his fingers to the bone, side by side with his men, had thought it all right to place an occasional wager, then how could it possibly be wrong?

She'd overheard Paul, in the feed and grain, telling Greta that the long dry spell had all but destroyed his corn crop. "It'll take a hundred dollars to see us through the winter," he'd admitted to the elderly shopkeeper, "and to buy enough seed for next year's crop, too." His broad shoulders had slumped as he'd added, in a weaker voice, "But I don't expect it to happen."

The money Valerie had been squirreling away was burning a hole in her bread box. If she put the money on the Mule Race, and won, Paul would have the money he needed!

Doc was honest, straightforward, and smart; as such, he had been chosen to keep an accurate record of the wagers. Valerie slipped into his office and slapped ten dollars on his desk. "I think Bertram's horse will win the race," she announced.

Leaning back in his squeaking swivel chair, Doc smiled. "That's a lot of money to lose if you're wrong—"

"I know that. But it isn't money I earned. It's money I found in Mama's Bible. I saved it all this time for an emergency...."

His brow furrowed with concern. "There's nothing wrong, is there, Miss Valerie?"

She put him at ease with a grin and a wave of her hand. "No, of course not." She didn't feel right telling Doc about Paul's money troubles. "It's just that if I win, I can put the money to good use." She clapped her hands. "Maybe for a store-bought wedding gown!"

Nodding with approval, Doc opened his ledger book and added her name to the list of bettors, then wrote the amount of her bet beside it. "Good luck," he said, holding out his hand.

Valerie shook it. "I don't really believe in luck," she said, smiling, "but thanks just the same."

The marching band had gathered on the hill overlooking Freeland Road and then marched down Oakland Road, right to the center of town, where the band members now surrounded the big, white gazebo in which Mayor Jenkins gave a long-winded "Why We're Thankful to Be Americans" speech. Then, Rev. Gemmill said grace, and the picnic began.

As the townsfolk ate, the gazebo became a stage where Jimmy Tucker did his juggling act, Tommy Morris showed his neighbors a few magic tricks, Billy Schuster played the banjo, and Marta Gemmill sang six country ballads, accompanying herself on the mandolin.

Just before one o'clock, the final preparations were underway for the big race. Horses and riders lined up in front of the black-smith's shop as a crowd gathered on either side of Main Street. Rev. Gemmill said a prayer for the safety of all the participants, and then the riders settled into their saddles.

"On your mark," Doc called, his starter pistol aimed at the fluffy, white clouds overhead, "get set...go!"

With whoops and hollers, the riders were off, leaving nothing behind but the curious onlookers and a cloud of dust. The course wound through the town and its outskirts like a wrinkled ribbon. There were six steep hills, two shallow streams, one rocky gorge, and a deep valley to cross before the riders hit the trail that ran alongside Middletown Road. When they crossed the finish line in about an hour, they'd have traveled fifteen miles.

Paul and Valerie left the starting line and rejoined the children in the picnic area behind the church. Together, the soon-to-be-complete family enjoyed slices of Greta's famous apple pie. The cheers and applause of most of the bettors, still gathered up and down Main Street as they awaited the winner, could be heard from where they were sitting at a table beneath a huge silver maple tree.

"I truly don't understand why a man would take his hard-earned money and bet it on something as frivolous as a horse race," Paul said around a mouthful of pie.

His angry expression and tone of voice made Valerie stop chewing. Was Paul really among those who thought betting was wrong?

As if he'd heard her thoughts, Paul said, "I say any man who'd do such a thing isn't just a fool—he's a sinner, to boot."

Valerie swallowed the mouthful of pie and stared at what remained of the slice before her. She'd never heard such venom in his voice. Obviously, he felt very strongly about this issue. What would he say if she won? Surely, he wouldn't accept any money that came his way by what he believed to be wrongful means.

And when he learned about her bet, what would he think of her? Would he break off their engagement, unable to yoke himself to a fool...and a *sinner*?

Valerie's smile vanished, and she pushed her pie plate away. Suddenly, she had no stomach for sweets.

Chapter Twelve

Politely, but without explanation, Valerie excused herself from the table. She sought out Doc in the crowd and, when she found him, grasped his hand and pulled him gently away from the group with whom he had been standing.

"Say, missy, what's goin' on?" the confused man asked.

"Paul—he said—he's...."

Doc's grin became a frown. "Is everything all right?"

Valerie sighed and plopped onto a nearby bench. "No, it's *not* all right. I'm a—I'm a *sinner!*"

Doc sat down beside her and patted her hand. "Now, what on earth would make you say a silly thing like that? When it comes to bein' *good*, why, you could write a book!"

She glanced over at the finish line. Soon, one rider would cross it, and if that rider was Bertram....

She sighed. "Paul doesn't believe in gambling, Doc. And I put ten whole dollars on that race," she said, her voice trembling.

Doc snickered. "Is that all?"

She met his clear, blue eyes. "Is that *all*? Why, it's *everything*. He said anyone who would bet his hard-earned money is a fool and a sinner. He'll think I'm...." She paused, wringing her hands. "He'll *know* what I am when he finds out what I've done. It won't matter that I did it for him. To a good Christian like Paul, a sin is a sin. Oh, my, what am I going to do?"

Doc took a deep breath. "You placed a bet for a man who doesn't believe in gambling...." He shook his graying head. "Help me understand this, Valerie."

"Well, of course I didn't know he opposed gambling when I placed the bet," she explained. "You see, I did it only because I heard him telling Greta he was worried about making it through the winter. It's been so dry this year...and the corn crop is so poor...and this year's corn would pay for next season's seed.... I just thought if I could get the money, if I helped him...."

"You're rambling, Miss Valerie," Doc teased, gently chucking her under the chin.

Valerie blinked back the tears stinging her eyelids. "What am I going to do, Doc?"

He put a reassuring arm around her. "I brought Paul into this world, Valerie, so you could say I've known him all his life. He's a kind man. Patient. I'm sure that when he hears the whole story, he'll understand."

"But what if he thinks he made a mistake when he asked me to marry him? What if he doesn't want a sinner raising his children? What if he breaks our engagement?"

Doc laughed. "If he does that, then *he's* the fool." After a moment, he added, "And a sinner, too."

Valerie frowned. "Paul? A sinner? Hardly."

"Waste not, want not," Doc said. "I can't think of a greater waste than to let a woman like you go, now that he's got you."

But Valerie seemed not to have heard the doctor's reassuring words. "I can't wallow in fear and self-pity a moment longer. I have to *do* something before I lose my mind!" She sat up straight and lifted her chin. "It'll be best if I tell him myself. Before the riders get back, rather than after...."

"Probably," Doc agreed.

"I suppose I should go and find him now."

"I suppose."

"Maybe he won't be as angry as I think...."

"Maybe."

She stood up and nervously brushed imaginary crumbs from her skirt. "I guess there's no time like the present."

"I guess."

She met her older friend's eyes. "Thanks, Doc."

"Hey, what are friends for?" Then, winking, he added, "And, speaking of friends, maybe you ought to hunt down the reverend, get his view of things before you meet up with Paul."

She nodded. "Good advice. Thanks again."

Doc watched Valerie walk away, her tiny shoulders squared, her narrow back straight as an arrow. From what he'd heard, she'd survived a lot of misery in her short life, yet she acted now as if this thing with Paul was the biggest adversity she'd ever faced. Doc knew this much: If Paul Collins did reject Valerie over this difference of opinion, he wasn't the man he'd always thought him to be.

Rev. Gemmill was sitting alone on the glider swing behind the gazebo when Valerie found him. A mouthful of his wife's pie caused his cheek to protrude. "Valerie," he said, swallowing. "Please, won't you join me?"

She sat down next to him and smoothed her skirt.

"My, my, my. What's got that pretty face all twisted in s... ess?"

Valerie sighed. It seemed she'd been doing a lot of that today. "I have a sin to confess—I think."

That inspired a quiet chuckle. "A sin...you *think?*"

Valerie nodded. "You see, I overheard Paul saying he needed money...." She leaned forward and whispered, "You'll keep that piece of information to yourself, of course...."

Smiling, Rev. Gemmill nodded. "Of course."

"Well, I had a little money saved up—not enough to see him through the winter, you understand—but enough. And I heard that some folks were betting on the Mule Race, and—"

The reverend held up his hand. "Let me guess: You placed a wager on...which, Bertram's horse?"

Valerie nodded.

"Well, first of all, let me say that if you're going to be a gambler, at least you're going to be a smart one. My daddy raised quarter horses, and I know something about 'em. And that filly of Bert's is a winner, for sure."

Valerie's heart fluttered. "Do you mean—"

"Now, don't misunderstand me. Just because I feel his horse will win doesn't mean I believe it's all right to place a bet on it."

Her heart sank.

"Gambling can be a dangerous thing. Like drink, it can tempt us into compulsions that are unhealthy—spiritually, emotionally, and bodily." He sat back and took a deep breath, then shook his head. "Now, I know there are those in town who don't believe there's a single thing wrong with placing an innocent little bet now and again. In fact, I happen to know that some of Freeland's most upstanding citizens do it regularly...though I'm sure they'd prefer to keep it secret from me," he added, smirking, "for fear I'd suggest the money would be better spent in the collection plate!"

Valerie explained her father's technique for gathering the tobacco harvest, hoping to justify why she'd done such an impetuous and foolish thing.

"Interesting. Very interesting. But here's the long and the short of it: In order for a gambler to win, everyone else must lose. Human nature dictates that somewhere deep inside, the gambler will actually begin to *hope* everyone else will lose so that he can collect the winnings, if you follow me.

"It's an issue of brotherly love, when you get right down to it. And what did Christ Jesus say about that? He said, '*Thou shalt love thy neighbour as thyself.*' Now, how can you love your neighbor at all if you're hoping against hope he'll lose his dollar so that you can win it?"

Valerie sighed again. The reverend was right, of course. Staring at her hands, folded primly in her lap, she shook her head, then looked up at him. "So, if a thing is wrong, then it's wrong always... and in all ways." She bit her lip to stop the tears that threatened. "Paul's right. I'm a fool and a sinner."

"Don't be so hard on yourself, child. Yours is more a sin of immaturity than a sin of evil. There's no question that you were misguided, just as there's no question that you did what you did to help the man you love."

The man you love, she repeated in her head.

Until today, Paul had loved her, too. She could only pray that, once she confessed everything to him, he'd love her enough to forgive her sin of covetousness.

"He's a good man," the reverend reminded her as she stood up to leave, "with a good and generous heart." He smiled gently. "Remember, in the truth, you'll find freedom."

Freedom in Freeland.

Ironic, she thought, that the first thing she saw when she looked away from his friendly face was the "Welcome to Freeland" sign that stood proudly in the town square.

Next, she saw Paul's tall silhouette headed straight toward her.

"Where on earth did you disappear to?" he wanted to know, wrapping her in a warm hug. "I've missed you!"

She found that she couldn't meet his eyes. Shame burned in her cheeks. "I've been...talking with friends," she answered.

"Is that so? Well, now it's time to talk to your future husband." He took her hand and led her to the courthouse steps. "I think it's high time we set a date. How would you feel about an autumn wedding?" he asked, sitting down on the top step and patting the space beside him.

She sat down. "Before I answer that, I've a confession to make."

Paul's quiet laughter soothed her—almost. "What could a sweet, young thing like you have to confess?"

She turned and faced him. "I think you should know, before we exchange lifetime vows, that you're linking yourself to a sinner. And a fool."

Confusion creased his brow.

"I'm afraid that—"

Just then, the hollering started. "They're coming!" someone shouted. "The riders are on their way!"

Paul jumped up and hurried down the brick courthouse steps. "Well, don't you want to see who'll win?"

She tucked in one corner of her mouth. "I'm not the least bit curious," she said sullenly.

"Well, come stand beside me, then, while I watch the winner cross the finish line." He held out his hand and waited until she put hers in it. "Go ahead," he said as they headed for the crowd. "Pick a winner, if you can."

"I'd really rather not."

"Don't be a spoilsport. Tell me who you think will win."

Valerie sighed. Again. "Bertram," she said dully. "I think Bert is going to win."

Paul nodded. "I agree. That filly of his is prime stock. Strong flanks. Good lines. Bert can surely use the prize money." He paused, then asked, "Since you're so astute at choosing winners, who'll come in second?"

"Josh's pony."

"Seriously?"

She nodded. "Almost as good as the quarter horse...."

"I think Josh will enjoy his new saddle." Then, almost as an afterthought, he said, "Know what I wish?"

Her heart swelled with love and admiration as she looked up at his handsome face. It hammered so loudly, in fact, that she barely heard the thundering hooves of the horses, just a mile or so from where they stood. "What do you wish?"

"I wish I had a fast horse."

"You would have entered the race?"

"Indeed, I would. But not for the money. Not for that saddle, either."

Valerie blinked, waiting for him to explain why he would have run the race.

"Third place would have been prize enough for me."

Third prize, she recalled, was dinner for two at the Freelander.

"I'd like nothing better than to treat you to a fancy evening out. You deserve only the best, you know."

The heart that had been pounding furiously skipped a beat. "No, that's where you're mistaken," she said.

"Does that nonsensical comment have anything to do with what you said back there at the courthouse about having a confession to make?"

Valerie nodded, and her heart went back to beating doubly fast.

He draped an arm over her shoulders. "Well, just for the record, no matter what you say, I'm gonna love you till the day I die."

She stood there, stiff and silent, praying it was true.

"Okay, spit it out. Tell me this awful thing that's been eating at you all afternoon."

Just then, Bertram blew by them on his prized horse, followed by Josh on his pony. One by one, the riders passed as the crowd applauded, cheered, and whistled through the thick cloud of street grit the horses had kicked up.

While everyone else ran over to congratulate the winners in front of the blacksmith's shop, Paul and Valerie hung back near the finish line.

"I love you, you know," he said quietly. "Nothing you say is going to change that."

Tears welled in her eyes, and a sob choked her words. How could she do this to him? How could she sentence him to a lifetime with a woman who knew so little about faith and spirituality and purity that she'd stupidly place a bet?

He deserved a woman with a good heart. A woman who knew the Bible as well as he did, so she could help instruct his children—and theirs, when they came along in the ways of the Lord. He deserved a devout, pious, Christian woman, not some bumbling, fumbling fool who'd childishly gamble in the hopes of turning a profit at the expense of her friends and neighbors!

"Valerie, you're crying. Tell me what's wrong, sweetheart. You know, if we're to be married, we should be able to tell each other anything...."

If we're to be married....

She wanted to tell him to go and find the woman he deserved, for that woman surely wasn't she. But a sob stuck tight in her throat, allowing no sound to escape.

Even if she could swallow and make it go away, the tears that spilled down her cheeks would prevent her from telling him what he needed to hear.

Valerie took great pride in the fact that she'd never been one to run from trouble. Instead, she consistently faced it head-on. So, it confused her as much as it did Paul when she turned and ran toward the shelter of her little cottage behind the schoolhouse.

She sat alone at her tiny kitchen table and stared at the pile of money for nearly an hour. What would she do with it? She couldn't give her winnings to Paul; he'd made it crystal-clear how he felt about gambling. She couldn't donate it to the church; Rev. Gemmill had been equally emphatic about ill-gotten gains. And she certainly had no intentions of keeping it for herself....

Perhaps Doc could use it to buy some newfangled surgical tool. Or supplies. Or medical books.

Josh might take it—hadn't he said last week that the cots in the jailhouse were infested with lice?

The schoolhouse could use a new blackboard. New arithmetic books. New readers....

Valerie shunned that idea; it would be too much like keeping the money for herself.

Maybe I ought to stand up on the water tower and let the bills rain down on Main Street. Let folks think it's like manna from heaven, she mused.

Darkness had begun to settle over the town. Valerie got up to light a lantern, and as she did, she spied the lovely rocking chair Paul had made for her. He was such a good and thoughtful man. Life with him would be beautiful.

But enough of that!

She'd decided to give him the greatest gift of her love: freedom from the likes of her. And she'd started immediately after the race, when he'd followed her home and knocked on her door with the all-out persistence of a man in love. He'd hollered that he loved her. That no matter what awful thing she wanted to tell him, he'd keep on loving her. He'd seemed oblivious to the puzzled stares of fellow Freelanders who'd heard and seen his deliberate banging as they'd passed by on their way home from the race. He'd yelled that he'd scraped his knuckles on the wooden door and had promised to start conking his noggin against it if she didn't open it soon, then had asked how that would look to the gaggle of people who had gathered to witness his temporary insanity.

Valerie hadn't opened the door.

She hadn't answered his many questions.

Instead, she'd sat in the chair he'd made for her, hugging her knees to her chest and weeping for the love, now gone, that her own stupidity had cost her.

It's best this way, she told herself. *Best for Paul, anyway. He'll find a decent, God-fearing woman to share his life with, and with her, he'll know the happiness he deserves.*

Could she stay in this town and watch him spend his life with another woman?

She didn't think so.

Sally and her husband, according to her cousin's last letter, had decided to remain in England indefinitely. So, she had no real family here. Still, could she leave Freeland, her new home, and all the wonderful friends she'd made?

Absolutely not.

There was only one thing to do, as she saw it. She'd done it before—many times. Like a soldier, she'd march onward with eyes straight ahead, chin up, shoulders back. *Stop your bellyaching and take your medicine like a big girl,* she told herself. *You're getting what you deserve, after all....*

But what, exactly, *did* she deserve? The compassion and friendship of a man like Paul Collins? The love and acceptance of his adorable children?

No; all of that added up to too much happiness.

And that kind of happiness, Valerie decided, was simply not in God's greater plan for her life. At least, not yet. She'd prayed about it, long and hard. And what answer had the Lord given her? She believed He knew her immature heart well; knew He had much to teach her about patience, tolerance, and love before she could be a proper wife and mother to anyone, let alone a man and children who had been tossed about by life's cruel winds. Much as she wanted to be part of the Collins family, she felt unworthy of such an important task.

The pain of resignation, much to Valerie's amazement, didn't infuriate her. Rather, she accepted the matter with grace and dignity. She'd never retreat into her angry, spiteful attitude toward the Lord again. Instead, she'd devote herself to spreading His Word.

She'd turn her whole life over to Him and His church. If she couldn't have Paul, she didn't want marriage and all the comforting warmth that came with it, anyway. If she couldn't have Paul, she didn't want children, either. She'd continue to be satisfied with loving and teaching the children of her friends and neighbors.

She slept fitfully as one thought repeatedly flitted through her mind: She couldn't have Paul. She couldn't have Paul. She couldn't have Paul....

Scruffy's tongue against her cheek woke her just as the sun was peeking over the horizon. Oblivious to the troubles of his mistress, the dog was letting her know that his stomach commanded attention. "All right," she said, drying her cheek with the back of her hand, "I'm up, and you'll soon have your breakfast. I promise."

Standing at the kitchen sink, Valerie raised and lowered the pump handle and filled the enamel pan beneath it with cool, clear water. After splashing her face with some water, she patted it dry with a blue gingham tea towel. The morning world always looked better after she'd freshened her face.

Grinning at her pet, Valerie scooped several spoonfuls of leftover stew into Scruffy's dish. "There," she said, ruffling his sandy-colored fur, "are you happy now?"

The dog barked in approval, then buried his muzzle in the meal.

Since school had officially ended for the summer back in June, Valerie passed her days puttering in her flower gardens and tending her vegetable plot. She'd painted the entire interior of her house white and the trim cornflower blue. She'd painted the outside white, too, and slapped a coat of maroon on the shutters, doors, and porch floors.

Today, she decided, slipping into a well-worn pink cotton dress, she'd wash the windows. For a small house, there were a lot of them. Twelve in all, each with twelve separate panes.

But first, she'd take down the filmy curtains and give them a good cleaning. While they dried on the clothesline out back, she'd tackle the glass.

Perched on a stepladder so that she could reach the top row of kitchen window panes, Valerie didn't hear the footsteps. The sound of his voice startled her so much that she nearly dumped the tin bucket of vinegar water on his head.

Paul placed a hand on each of the ladder's support rails. "Now, I've got you where I want you," he said, "and you're not going anywhere until you talk to me."

Valerie wanted nothing more than to dive into his strong arms. To tell him what a silly little fool she'd been to place a bet. To beg his forgiveness and promise never to do such an un-Christian thing like gamble again.

But she knew herself too well. She'd always been impetuous. Quick to jump to conclusions. Too fast to make judgments. These were character traits that would, in all likelihood, be a part of her till the day she died. She couldn't subject Paul to spending the rest of his life with a human seesaw.

"I'm very busy, Paul."

"Yes," he said, his voice tinged with impatience, "I can see that. But the windows will wait. I will not."

"The almanac says it may rain tomorrow," she explained. "I want to get this job done today, so that—"

"I don't care what the almanac says." Anger rang in his voice and ebbed from his dark eyes. "Valerie Ann Carter, you will come down off that ladder right this minute, or I'll come up and *bring* you down."

Chapter Thirteen

B ut Pa misses you so," Tricia said.

Tears welling in the girl's pale eyes prompted Valerie to reach out and wrap her in a warm, protective embrace. "Your pa will be fine, in time," Valerie whispered, placing a kiss atop her blonde mop of curls. "You'll see."

"That's what folks said when Ma died. But he wasn't fine. Not fine at all. He was sad. So sad—all the time." Tricia pulled away from the hug to stare deep into Valerie's eyes. "It was *you* who made him happy again."

Valerie sighed. Paul had said as much during his last visit to her house. After much convincing, she'd come down off the ladder and gone into the kitchen with him. After much convincing, she'd listened quietly as he told her what he'd heard from Doc and Rev. Gemmill. After much convincing, she'd almost believed it didn't matter one whit to him that she'd placed a bet—something that by his standards was sinful and reprehensible.

She'd almost believed it….

And then it had been his turn to sit silently as she attempted to convince him what must be. "You deserve a good Christian woman," she'd said. "Someone who knows right from wrong, who knows without even thinking about it what the good Lord wants from her."

His left eyebrow had arched as one corner of his mouth had turned down. "Sometimes, for a woman who's so smart, you can say some very stupid things."

Valerie had gotten angry at that, and had stood so quickly that her chair had nearly tipped over. She'd refilled his glass with lemonade—not to be a good hostess, but to keep from slapping that look of righteous indignation off his face.

"Sit back down here and show me the courtesy, at least, of helping me understand what on God's green earth you're talking about," he'd insisted, pointing to her empty chair.

When she'd sat down, he'd added, "You say you were raised in a devout Christian household. You say you know the Bible inside and out." He'd grabbed her hands in his and peered deep into her eyes. "If you're so all-fired knowledgeable in the Word, why is it that you don't know the good Lord isn't judging you as a sinner for one minor transgression?"

On her feet again, Valerie had paced the space between the kitchen table and the back door. "It's not God's judgment I fear!" she'd snapped. "*You* taught me that His love forgives human error. What I did—that silly bet—it was a mistake. A misunderstanding, plain and simple." She'd stood still then, pointing her finger at him. "It's *you* I can't bear to face, Paul Collins. It's your perfect manner of living, your code of honor that scares the daylights out of me! I'm not as good as you, Paul. I'll never be able to live up to your standards. I'll be a constant source of disappointment to you."

Then, he'd gotten on his feet, too, fists resting on his hips as he faced her. His laughter, bitter and soft, had grated in her ears. "I'll say this for you, Valerie: you sure know how to hurt a man."

"But...." Valerie had blinked and looked from his wounded expression toward the door, outside of which was freedom from his pain. "But hurting you is exactly what I'm trying to *prevent*," she'd confessed. "I'm not good for you, Paul. I'm too…too ghty. Too unsettled. Too immature to be the wife of any man, let alone a man with three needy children to raise. Too…."

"Too busy feeling sorry for herself," he'd interrupted her, "to see what's right under your nose."

He'd taken one step forward, closing the gap that separated them, and placed a hand on her shoulder. The fingertip of his free hand had lifted her chin, forcing her to meet his gaze. "I love you," he'd said, his voice raspy with emotion. "I love you because you have a heart the size of your head. Because you lived through terror and anguish, and you *survived*. You thrived and flourished in spite of it.

"I love you because you taught my children it was right and good to miss their mother, that laughing and loving again couldn't diminish her memory."

He'd held her close and whispered into her hair, "I love you because you taught *me* it was right and good to love again."

Then, Paul had held her at arm's length, his dark eyes boring intently into her green ones. "You're dead wrong when you say I'm perfect. I'm far from it. Just as you're wrong about that, you're right when you say you're not perfect. Believe it or not, I love *that* about you most of all. I can't imagine spending the rest of my days permanently bound to a woman who's insufferably perfect!"

Holding her close again, he'd added, "I won't lie to you, Valerie; I don't approve of gambling. But I certainly haven't judged you a sinner because you placed one bet. Don't you see?" he'd asked, tenderly taking her face in his hands. "Don't you *see*," he'd repeated, "that I love you for the *reason* you placed that bet?"

Valerie hadn't been able to speak. Not in the presence of such pure, sweet love. Never before had a man looked at her with such complete trust. Such total admiration. Never before had a man put his heart in her hands for safekeeping. And never before had she felt more unworthy.

He was, by far, the best man she'd ever known. And, as such, he deserved only the best.

Everyone—including Doc, Rev. Gemmill, and God Himself—knew that the best was not Valerie Carter! Everyone, that is, but Paul. Somehow, she had to make him face that fact....

"Do you think I'd lie to you, Valerie?"

Blinking, she'd shaken her head. She'd known that he'd sooner cut off a limb than tell a deliberate falsehood.

"Do you think I'd ever do anything to harm you in any way?"

Again, she'd shaken her head.

"So, you trust me, then?"

"With my very life," she'd whispered. And she'd meant it, all the way down to the marrow of her bones.

"Then believe me when I say I love you. How much I owe to you!"

She'd walked a few steps away. "You owe me nothing. Nothing."

"Ah," he'd said, standing so close behind her that she'd felt his breath in her hair, "you're wrong. Dead wrong. I owe to you my children's happiness."

He'd turned her around and cupped her chin in his palm. "I owe to you my happiness."

How would she make him see that if she could so completely misunderstand God's Word regarding gambling, she might just as easily misunderstand some other important message in His Word? What if she transmitted that misunderstanding to the children? To those innocent, loving children, who looked to Paul—who would look to her, as their new mother—for guidance and instruction?

And what if that misunderstanding led one of them astray? Valerie couldn't allow it to happen. *Wouldn't* allow it to happen.

She'd looked into Paul's wide, brown eyes—eyes so full of love for her that it had made her heart ache—and said what she felt had to be said: "Go home, Paul. Go home to your children. Go home and pray long and hard on this 'love' you declare you feel for me. I think you'll soon discover, with God's help, that it's not love at all but mere infatuation."

She'd patted his hand, much in the same way she'd comfort a student who couldn't figure out a difficult arithmetic problem. "In time, the Lord will introduce you to the woman He feels is worthy of you; the woman who'll be a dedicated and devoted wife to you; the woman He believes will be a good role model, a good influence, a good teacher of His Word…for your *children*."

"He's already shown me that woman."

He'd said it so quickly, so matter-of-factly, that it had stunned her into silence.

After a few moments, she'd taken a deep breath and walked purposefully to the door. Opening it, she'd stood with one hand on the knob and gestured toward the back porch. "Go home, Paul," she'd said again. "Get on with your life, and let me get on with mine. Please…."

He'd taken a few uncertain steps toward the opening but had stopped when they'd been side by side. "Give me a little credit, why don't you?" he'd said, anger brewing in his voice. "Don't you think I've already considered how a marriage between us would affect my children? Don't you think I've prayed long into the night whether or not you'd be a good mother? They've suffered enough, God knows. I certainly don't want to subject them to more.

"Don't you think I've asked for His guidance to show me whether or not you'd be a good wife? I'm not an idiot, Valerie. I made a good choice, for all the right reasons, and with God's blessing, I might add!"

Valerie had only been able to stare at the pointy toes of her black boots.

"All right," he'd said softly. "I'll go. But not in search of 'some other woman,' as you say I should." He'd pulled his cap over his head and walked out onto the porch. "I'll not find such a woman anywhere on this earth," he'd added, facing her, "because there *is* no woman for me but you." He'd started down the steps. "When you come to your senses," he'd said, his jaw set in determination, "you know where to find me."

He'd stopped at the end of her walk. "Be careful what you ask for, Valerie, or you might get it." With that, he'd been gone.

The same determined look that had been etched on Paul's face that morning was now evident on his daughter's lovely face. "You told me you loved him," Tricia said, bringing Valerie back into the present. "Wasn't it true? Have you changed your mind? Have you met someone else?"

"Of course not!" Valerie exclaimed. "There's no one like your father!"

Tricia sighed and shrugged. "Then, I don't understand."

How would Valerie explain to this eager-eyed young girl that, while she loved her father more than life itself, she couldn't yoke him to life with one who continually fell from the path of righteousness? How would she tell this innocent, budding young woman that, though she'd like nothing more than to spend the rest of her life with a man as good and decent as Paul Collins, she couldn't subject him to the ups and downs of a marriage to a backsliding Christian?

"Do you love him?"

It was a simple enough question, and Valerie searched for an equally simple answer.

"Well, do you?" Tricia pressed.

"Yes, I love him," Valerie admitted.

"How much do you love him?"

She met the girl's gaze. How much? *More than all the stars in the heavens. More than all the grains of sand on all the world's beaches. More than all the tea in China!* Valerie thought.

"Do you love him enough to make sacrifices?"

"Sacrifices?"

"Pa says when you love someone—*really* love someone—you sometimes have to put your own needs and feelings aside and do what's best for that person."

Valerie frowned. "I'm afraid I'm not following you, Tricia."

The girl sighed again. "You know that he loves you; you say you love him."

Valerie nodded. "Yes...."

"Well, he needs you, too. Maybe he needs you more than he'd ever admit to anybody. Even to you. You're what's best for Pa. Can't you see that?"

Valerie took the girl's hands in her own. She was touched that Tricia wanted her as a mother as much as she wanted to fill the role. "Don't you see, Tricia, that your pa deserves a good wife? And you and Tyler and Timmy deserve a good mother? I honestly don't know if I'm up to the task."

"Pa said God sent you to him. He said he prayed and prayed, and you were the answer to his prayers."

Valerie's heart fluttered. *He said that to his children?*

"Me an' the boys, we prayed the same prayer," Tricia added. "God didn't send us Miss Watson or Miss Hunter. God sent us *you*."

Later that evening, and long into the night, Valerie thought about everything Tricia had said. On the one hand, she felt honored to be called the answer to the heartfelt prayers of this fine man and his children. On the other hand, she cringed under the weighty responsibility of it. "Lord," she prayed aloud, "help me. Show me how to do what's best for them...."

Valerie had been praying the same prayer nonstop, it seemed, for nearly a week, yet she hadn't heard God's answer. *The Lord must be trying to teach me a lesson in patience,* she told herself. *Isn't it amazing? The thing I do worst is the thing I'm expected to do most: wait.*

She was standing at the counter at Greta's feed and grain, waiting to pay for her purchases, when she looked through the window to see a black cloud roll in over the store, darkening the sky that had brightened its interior. "Dis could be one dangerous storm," Greta observed, stuffing Valerie's purchases into a box. "I hope no harm vill come to der farmers' fields."

Valerie nodded. She remembered that in Richmond, hard rains and high winds could cause more damage than just about anything to the tobacco crops. Throw in some lightning, and the threat of fire only made matters worse.

A loud clap of thunder caused Greta to squeal with fright. "Goodness!" she said. "Dat one vas too close for comfort! If der lightning follows soon behind, ve could be in trouble."

Valerie picked up her box and started toward the door. "Say a little prayer that I'll get home before trouble starts," she said over her shoulder, grinning as she left the store.

Greta followed her out onto the narrow porch. "You kin bet dat I vill," she said, nudging Valerie's shoulder playfully with her own.

Paul's wagon was parked outside the blacksmith's shop, loaded with sacks of flour, cornmeal, and sugar. His children were sitting in the wagon bed, and when they saw Valerie, all three shouted hello and waved.

Smiling, Valerie returned their friendly greeting. She hadn't seen Tricia since the week before, when the girl had demanded an explanation for the distance between her father and her teacher. As she neared the wagon, Valerie hoped that the subject of their separation wouldn't come up, for she still had no reasonable excuse for calling a halt to the engagement—at least, none that would appease the curious girl.

"Pa's inside," Timmy told her as she stepped alongside the wagon, "getting a new wheel made. He's gonna fix up the carriage."

Valerie remembered how he'd spent many a spare moment repairing the upholstery and fringe on the surrey he'd found in the barn upon his return to Freeland. "I have a lot of incentive to restore it now," he'd told her. "I want to whisk you away from the church in it on our wedding day...."

Suddenly, the children, who'd been lounging among the over-stuffed, white cloth bags, bolted upright at another booming roll of thunder. "Look at that!" Timmy shouted, pointing at the horizon. "Smoke!"

Everyone's gaze followed his chubby forefinger. "Why, that's Bert's farm!" Greta exclaimed. "Lord above," she prayed, "let it be chust a tree dat's burning over dere...."

Thunder pealed a third time, louder than ever. Tricia's high-pitched scream echoed up and down Main Street.

In her fearful response to the scream, Sadie, Paul's big black mare, whinnied and reared up on her hind legs, loosing the reins, which were tethered to the hitching post. The wagon lurched forward precariously, then tipped up, up, until Tyler and Tricia were spilled out the back, along with the bags of feed and grain. Only Timmy remained on the wagon bed, clutching the rough-hewn sideboards.

"Pa!" Tyler shouted. "Pa, come quick! Sadie's gonna run off with Timmy!"

But Paul couldn't hear the boy's cries over the shrill sounds of the grinder's wheel deep in the bowels of the blacksmith's shop.

Valerie swiftly set down her box and moved quickly to the right side of the wagon, saying a silent prayer of thanks that the brake was still set. But Sadie's wild eyes and glistening flanks showed her fear. If she were allowed to continue bucking and pitching, she'd splinter the brake—and rush onward, taking Timmy with her. *No telling where she'll go in the state she's in*, Valerie realized.

She had to do something, and do it fast.

But what?

Valerie scrambled up into the wagon seat. As always, Paul had wound the leather leads around the brake handle. Quickly, Valerie unwound them and pulled back with all her might. "Whoa, Sadie!" she hollered. "Whoa, there!"

For a fraction of a second, it seemed like Sadie would respond. The horse, on all fours now, bobbed her head up and down and snorted. She'd just begun to quiet when another thunderbolt crashed.

Again, Sadie reared up, whinnying for all she was worth.

It seemed to Valerie that the next moments took half an hour to pass. First, she heard the sickening, cracking sounds that told her the brake handle was beginning to splinter. Next came the unmistakable groan of the wheels as the huge, heavy wagon began to move forward.

She'd wrapped the reins tightly around her hands, and the leather dug mercilessly into her flesh as the horse strained against the bit. "Whoa, Sadie!" Valerie shouted again. "Easy there, girl."

Sadie had had just about enough of the hustle and bustle of the storm. And she'd go home, lickety-split, if not for the tugging of one stubborn female in her master's seat.

This time, however, stubbornness couldn't win out over animal strength.

The suddenness of Sadie's forward motion flung Valerie from the driver's seat.

She clung for several frightening seconds to the underside of the wagon, her feet dragging and scraping along the gravelly grit of Main Street before she managed to pull herself back up into the wagon again.

The wagon hadn't been built for high speeds, even on smooth streets such as Freeland's. Soon, though, Valerie realized, they'd be on the road leading out of town...a road gouged with deep, rain-washed crevices and littered with large rocks that had been washed down from the hillside in the last big rain.

The last of Freeland's buildings whizzed by. Trees, distant farm-houses, barns, and pasturelands whirred past at a dizzying pace. A few minutes at this speed, and the wagon would fall apart completely.

A quick glance back told Valerie that Timmy's hold on the wagon wall was precarious, at best. A few more jolts, and his tiny hands would let go of the graying boards; a few more jolts, and he'd be sent sailing over those boards....

Valerie couldn't bear to think about where he'd land. She had to stop the wagon—or die trying. Timmy's life depended on it.

The steel bars on either side of Sadie kept her attached to her heavy burden. They looked strong. Stable. Secure. Could Valerie step out on one of them and manage to climb on Sadie's back? She'd been an able horsewoman in Richmond.... If she could climb aboard, would she be strong enough to force the terrified horse to stop?

Another glance back....

Where's Timmy?

She saw a lot in her next quick glance: a trickle of blood oozing from his forehead. Closed eyes. Limp limbs. *He's unconscious!* "Timmy!" Valerie screamed. "Timmy, can you hear me?"

The boy's eyes remained closed, and his little body flopped about with the movements of the wagon like a rag doll. Whether or not she could accomplish the feat was no longer a question. If she didn't succeed, Timmy would pay the price.

Valerie gathered up her flowing, blue gingham skirts and tucked them into the wide, matching cloth belt at her waist. Holding tightly to the driver's footrest, she placed one booted foot on the bar nearest her, then stepped out with the other foot, trying to remain steady on the vibrating metal.

Valerie's slight weight was still enough to tilt the harness and cause Sadie to turn off the road. The horse was running full throttle across the wide field alongside Freeland Road, and if she kept up at this pace, and in this direction, she'd run straight into Walker's Gorge. By Valerie's quick estimate, she had less than thirty seconds to jump onto Sadie's back and pull her to a halt, or Timmy, the wagon...all of them would plummet to their deaths at the bottom of the gorge.

"Lord," she prayed through clenched teeth, "grant me the strength to do what I must...."

To get from her tentative foothold on the harness to Sadie's back required a leap of nearly a yard—no small feat in a speeding, runaway wagon. If she missed....

Valerie couldn't think about that. It was a risk she had to take.

And so, she jumped, hands outstretched to grasp the straps cinched beneath Sadie's round belly. It seemed to take minutes, rather than seconds, to fly that short distance; it seemed her fingers would never close around the leather loops. But, finally, she was there, astride the big horse's broad back, grasping Sadie's mane like a lifeline.

"Whoa, Sadie!" she shouted. "Pull back, girl! Stop!"

With her hands full of the horse's soft hair, Valerie leaned back as far as the length of her arms would allow. "Let it be far enough, Lord…. Please, let it be enough…."

Sadie's thick neck tensed. Her head went high. Then, as suddenly as she'd started the journey on Main Street, she came to a dead halt.

Panting, Valerie hugged the horse's sweaty neck. Tears stung her eyes.

"What's goin' on?" called a panicked voice.

"Timmy!" Valerie shouted, turning around. "Praise the Lord, you're all right!"

He rubbed his head. "Guess I must'a cracked my skull some back there," he said, gesturing toward the town with a jerk of his tiny thumb. "Guess we oughtta get back before we're soaked to the skin," he added, blinking raindrops from his big, frightened eyes.

Valerie had been so busy trying to get from the wagon to Sadie's back that she hadn't even noticed that it had begun to rain. Huge, round drops plopped to the ground all around them, scattering dust, at first, and then matting it down in sodden puddles.

Slowly, so as not to spook Sadie again, Valerie slid to the ground, then climbed up into the wagon seat. "C'mon, Sadie," she said, gently urging the horse to turn around and head back to town. "Let's go home."

Chapter Fourteen

You saved his life," Paul said, wrapping Timmy in a big, protective hug.

Blushing, Valerie grinned and brushed a wayward curl from her forehead.

Paul reached out and grasped her hand. "Look at you—you're bleeding!"

Only then did she notice that both her hands were swollen, raw, and bloody from straining against the reins. "I read that the folks who have settled out in the Wild West call newcomers 'tenderfeet' because they haven't developed calluses to protect them from the hot, sandy soil." Giggling nervously and winking at Timmy, Valerie added, "I guess you can just call me Tender Fingers from now on."

"Tender Fingers. That's funny," Timmy said, laughing around the red lollipop Doc had given him.

Paul still held her hand in his own. "You risked your life for him." His voice was hoarse with relief and gratitude. "You're a— well, a hero, that's what you are."

Blushing, Valerie protested, "I did what anyone would have."

Paul shook his head. "From what Greta says, the street was filled with people, some of 'em big, strappin' men. None of them climbed into that wagon...or onto Sadie's back." He looked at her for a silent moment. "But *you* did."

Paul stood up from where he'd been sitting with Ti   y on
the squeaky cot in Doc's office, pulling Valerie up next to him.
"That was quite a gamble you took out there," he said, nodding
toward the door.

"I suppose it was a risk, since I don't know much about driving
a wagon."

His smile glimmered brightly in his eyes. "But I'll bet you
know more now than you knew thirty minutes ago."

She squeezed his hand gently and winced at the discomfort
the slight pressure caused her swollen, bruised fingers.

His brow furrowed with concern as he studied her hands. "To
merely say thank you doesn't seem appropriate at all. Not after the
chance you took…."

Gamble? Bet? Chance? Was he saying what she thought he
was saying?

"I always believed gambling was a sin, cut and dry. No excep-
tions," he said, interrupting her thoughts. "Imagine my surprise—
the son of a preacher learning such a lesson. And at my advanced
age!"

Valerie giggled. "Listen to you! You make it sound as if you're
as old as Father Time. Why, you're just a young whippersnapper!"

"Your sense of humor won't buy your way out of this one," Paul
said, pulling her close. "You gambled with your own life to save my
son's. There's nothing funny about that."

"Pa's right, Miss Carter," Timmy said. "You saved my life."

Paul laughed. "Tim, you're going to have to figure out something else to call her. It doesn't seem right calling your pa's wife
'Miss Carter,' now, does it?"

Timmy shook his head and gave the matter a moment's
thought. His tiny brow wrinkled under the white bandage Doc

had wrapped around his head. "D'you think Ma would mind if I called Miss Carter 'Ma'?"

Paul's smile seemed to warm the entire room as he looked from his son to Valerie and back again. "I'm sure she'd give her full approval." Then, he focused his attention on Valerie when he said, "What do you think, Miss Carter? Is it all right if my young'uns call you 'Ma'?"

Her heart was beating so furiously, Valerie thought it might leap right out of her chest. "It would be an honor," she said quietly. "But Paul, I need to explain…… I misinterpreted things so badly. I'd never read anything in the Bible that indicated gambling was a sin. Rev. Gemmill explained it all, so, now, I know better."

"That's because there's nothing specific in the Good Book that tells us whether it's right or wrong."

She slumped into Doc's wheeled armchair and sighed. "Still, I misunderstood the essence of God's Word. What if I do it again? And what if some stupid, silly, spur-of-the-moment thing I do leads the children away from God's path?"

Paul knelt before her and held her face in his hands, then silenced her with a soft, lingering kiss. "Nothing like that is going to happen. I know it like I know…like I know your name."

"Mrs. Paul Collins," Timmy said. "*That'll* be her name after the weddin', right, Pa?"

"Right, son."

"When's the weddin', Pa?"

Paul never took his eyes from Valerie's. "As soon as we can get Rev. Gemmill to agree to perform the ceremony."

"Tomorrow?" Timmy asked.

"Tonight, if I thought it was possible."

Valerie's eyes filled with tears. "Even though I—"

"The money will be mighty handy, come planting time," he said, interrupting her.

She looked at their hands.

"So, Valerie…what did you do with the money?"

It was all she could do to hide her grin. "Why, I put in the collection plate."

Paul's jaw dropped. "You did *what?*"

She met his gaze and smiled. "I knew you wouldn't want it—"

"But—"

"Gambling is for fools and sinners!"

He gathered her into his arms and pulled her to her feet. "Do you think the reverend can fit us in next Saturday?"

Nodding happily, Valerie sniffed.

"Can I tell Tyler and Tricia 'bout the weddin', Pa?"

In place of an answer, Paul pressed his lips to Valerie's and distractedly motioned his son out the door with a wave of his hand.

Moments later, all three Collins children were peering through the wide window in Doc's office. "I have a feeling we'll be playin' follow the leader down the center aisle in church real soon," Tyler said, grinning.

"Real soon," Tricia agreed, her hands folded over her chest.

"That's fine with me," Timmy said. "Follow the leader is my fav'rite game."

"Mine, too, Timmy," Valerie echoed. "Mine, too."

About the Author

A prolific writer, Loree Lough has more than seventy books, sixty short stories, and 2,500 articles in print. Her stories have earned dozens of industry and Reader's Choice awards. A frequent guest speaker for writers' organizations, book clubs, private and government institutions, corporations, college and high school writing programs, and more, Loree has encouraged thousands with her comedic approach to "learned-the-hardway" lessons about the craft and industry.

For decades, Loree has been an avid wolf enthusiast, and she dedicates a portion of her income each year to efforts that benefit the magnificent animals. She splits her time between a home in the Baltimore suburbs and a cabin in the Allegheny Mountains. She shares her life and residences with a spoiled pointer named Cash and her patient, dedicated husband, Larry, who has supported her writing and teaching endeavors throughout the years.

Loree loves hearing from her readers, so feel free to write her at loree@loreelough.com. To learn more about Loree and her books, visit her Web site at www.loreelough.com.